Praise for *The Royers of Renfrew*

"Having read the first two books of this trilogy I can hardly wait for the third one! . . . They bring the members of the Royer family to life in a way that gives the reader a feeling of being there in late 18th and early 19th century Pennsylvania . . . These books should be on everyone's library shelf."

- Carroll Martin -

"*Threads of Change* is a fabulous weaving of history and emotions! Felt like I was with Susan as she tried to make sense of her changing world . . . just love *The Royers of Renfrew* and look forward to the next chapter in their lives."

- Gay Fischetti Hollowell -

" . . . *Threads of Change* continues the saga of life at Renfrew from 1812 to 1815. . . You can close your eyes and imagine yourself being right there at the four-square garden, playing down by the creek, hopping in the wagon to go into town and doing many of the other daily tasks that need to be done . . ."

- William S. Domitrovich -

" . . . I grew attached to the Royers and continued to think about them even as I finished with this marvelous story! An endearing story of childhood friendships, sibling rivalries and neighbors helping neighbors. I can't wait for the next installment."

- Sue Noreen -

" . . . Through times of both great tragedy and great joy, the family's values of faith, hard work, self-sufficiency, and personal responsibility offer stark contrast to the dependency of much of contemporary American culture. An absorbing and fascinating read that places our own lives in far greater perspective . . ."

- Donald Bruce Foster, MD -
Author, *Kiss Tomorrow Goodbye*

Also by Maxine Beck and Marie Lanser Beck

The Royers of Renfrew – A Family Tapestry

The Royers of Renfrew – Threads of Change

The Royers of Renfrew

The Fabric of Life

Maxine Beck and Marie Lanser Beck

We do not live an equal life, but one of contrast and patchwork; now a joy, then a sorrow . . .

- Ralph Waldo Emerson

This is a work of fiction. Though many aspects are based on historical record, the work as a whole is a product of the authors' imaginations.

Little Antietam Press, LLC

Published in the United States

Dedication

Dedicated to the staff and volunteers of Renfrew Institute for Cultural and Environmental Studies and Renfrew Museum and Park in grateful appreciation for their interpretation of, and care for the historic house and farmstead that were the inspiration for our story.

Acknowledgements

"Many hands make work light" is a well-known Pennsylvania German expression. This was never more true than in the creation of our works of historical fiction. All three volumes of *The Royers of Renfrew* have drawn heavily upon the support, encouragement and practical assistance by numerous individuals who are devoted to Renfrew Museum and Park and the educational programming of the Renfrew Institute for Cultural and Environmental Studies.

Our storytelling and the presentation of this fictionalized account of the Royers 19th century lives would not have been possible without the guidance, assistance, encouragement and loving attention freely given by family, friends and colleagues.

The Royers of Renfrew has benefitted mightily by early readings by gifted editor Dennis Shaw; advice and recommendations by author and former Washington County Museum of Fine Arts Curator Jean Woods and Bonnie Iseminger of Renfrew Museum and Park. Melodie Anderson-Smith and Dr. Doris Goldman of the Renfrew Institute for Cultural and Environmental Studies, who were instrumental in the creation of Renfrew's four-square garden – the inspiration for this work of fiction – offered information and guidance.

We are indebted to Ruth Gembe for her encyclopedic knowledge of Franklin County history and the many families who have called this area home; to Linda Zimmerman who helped us navigate German usage, and proved to be a gifted proofreader in her own right, and to Renfrew Institute's Board President Wayne Martz's and Renfrew volunteer Andrea Struble's careful reading.

Betsy Domitrovich, a former Waynesboro resident and longtime volunteer at the Royer Mansion in Williamsburg, PA, enthusiastically supplied information about the Royers, who moved to Huntingdon County and provided photographs and resources that chronicle the iron ore industry to the north and west of us. Bill Spigler kindly loaned us his treasured copy of *Biographical Annals of Franklin County* for our research.

Nearly all of what we learned about dairy farming in the early 1800s came from longtime agricultural educator Gerald W. Reichard, his son Gerald J. Reichard, and Shippensburg veterinarians Dr. John C. Simms and Dr. Nadine Oakley. Their expertise and loan of an 1892 U.S.

Department of Agriculture *Special Report on Diseases of Cattle* proved most instructive.

RuthE Showalter, of Waynesboro, gave us insight into family relationships in Plain communities, and we appreciate many other readers who posed questions and suggestions that informed our narrative.

Waynesboro's Alexander Hamilton Memorial Free Library enabled us to access sources far afield through inter-library loan. In writing about Snow Hill Cloister we value particularly the work of the late Charles M. Treher and his pioneering history of that Pietist community published by the Pennsylvania German Society in 1968, and Denise A. Seachrist's book *Snow Hill: In the Shadows of the Ephrata Cloister* (Kent State University Press, 2010).

We were further aided in the description of the workings of 19th century iron ore furnaces and the impact on our region by the work of Stan Haas, who has done much to preserve knowledge about this important chapter in Franklin County history. Retired Shippensburg veterinarian Dr. John W. Fague's book *Do You Remember?* (2001) helped with details of Pennsylvania farm life in our area.

Andrew Gehman provided his talent for the cover photography, and Maxine Beck produced the interior illustrations. Special assistance in staging our cover photo was enthusiastically given by longtime board member Red Monn, Institute employees Tracy Holliday, Sherry Hesse, Pam Rowland and Dr. Doris Goldman and Ruth Gembe, who loaned the authentic Franklin County woven coverlet used in some of the photos.

Special thanks goes to niece Monica Beck who was the model for the cover, and to our business manager Stephen Beck. We also appreciate the encouragement in our foray into publishing from Waynesboro Hospital emergency room physician and author Dr. D. Bruce Foster.

Any errors in our recreation of life on the Royer farmstead and fictionalized events at Snow Hill Cloister and Old Forge are clearly our own, but we hope that visitors who wander Renfrew's 107 acres today will have a better appreciation for the trials and triumphs of the Pennsylvania Germans who tamed a wild land in an effort to fashion a livelihood for their families and find religious freedom.

Maxine Beck and Marie Lanser Beck
Waynesboro, Pennsylvania
September 2013

Authors' Notes

A Note on Religion

Religion played a major role in every aspect of the lives of Pietist Pennsylvania Germans who fled Europe to escape religious persecution. The Bible was the primary book governing their lives, and devotion to their principles and their community of believers was central to their daily lives. Children were given religious instruction in their homes from an early age and everything from the layout of the four-square garden to the religious holidays that determined the planting of crops was influenced by the dictates of their conservative pacifist Protestant sect.

A Note on Language

At the time of this narrative, the Royers would have spoken German exclusively in their home. But given their farmstead's role in the commerce of Waynesburg and the region, family members had contact with their English-speaking neighbors and needed to be able to communicate.

In addition, many newspapers and almanacs were published in German to cater to the many German settlers in the mid-Atlantic region. These publications were readily available to Daniel Royer and his family. Both the girls and boys in the Royer household were taught to read and write in German.

In this narrative, German phrases and expressions have been included to give the reader a sense of the sound and rhythm of the German spoken by the Royers and among the Pennsylvania Germans who, though most heavily concentrated in Pennsylvania, also settled in parts of Maryland and Virginia. These selected words and phrases are in italics to help the reader differentiate them from the rest of the text.

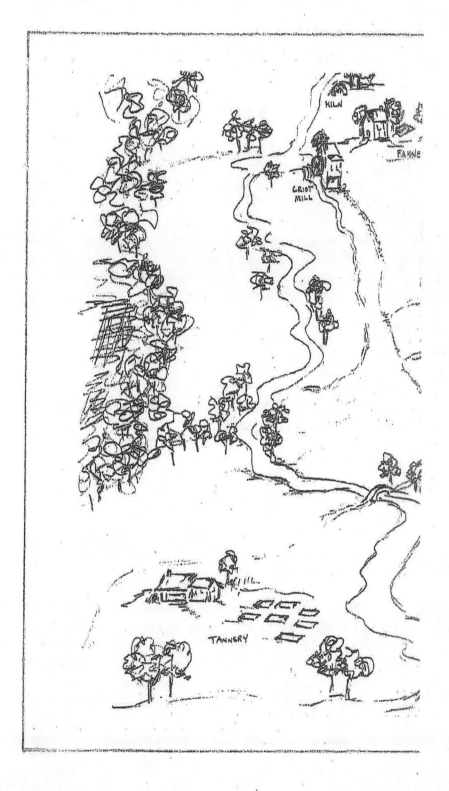

The Daniel Royer Family - 1821

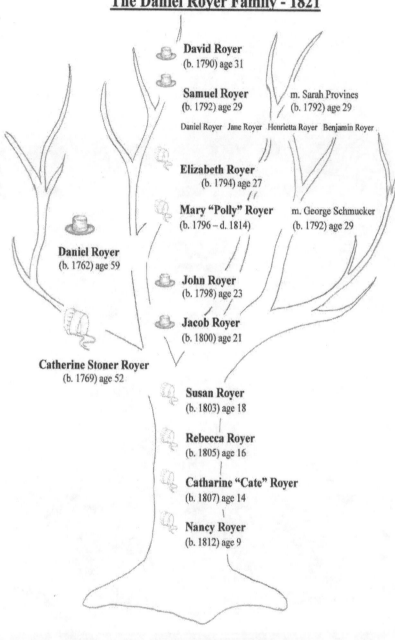

David Royer
(b. 1790) age 31

Samuel Royer   m. Sarah Provines
(b. 1792) age 29   (b. 1792) age 29

Daniel Royer   Jane Royer   Henrietta Royer   Benjamin Royer

Elizabeth Royer
(b. 1794) age 27

Mary "Polly" Royer   m. George Schmucker
(b. 1796 – d. 1814)   (b. 1792) age 29

Daniel Royer
(b. 1762) age 59

John Royer
(b. 1798) age 23

Jacob Royer
(b. 1800) age 21

Catherine Stoner Royer
(b. 1769) age 52

Susan Royer
(b. 1803) age 18

Rebecca Royer
(b. 1805) age 16

Catharine "Cate" Royer
(b. 1807) age 14

Nancy Royer
(b. 1812) age 9

Contents

Authors' Notes

Family Changes – Fall 1821

Susan Royer laid the sock she was darning in her lap and stretched her legs into the halo of flickering firelight of the large  kitchen hearth. The short ribbons of the small, white bonnet poised just above a bun of honey-brown hair fell across her shoulders. Rippling her toes against the knitted wool socks she had reluctantly scooped from the back of the dresser drawer that morning, she lamented, "Fall seems to fly by faster every year." She studied the nearly bare branches of the farmstead's old oaks silhouetted against the evening sky framed by the front window.

"Best get used to it," said her mother, Catherine, as she drew the floss through her latest embroidery piece. "The older you get, the faster time goes – and the slower *you* go." She set aside her needle and hoop and rubbed the swollen knuckles of her hands.

"But I'm only 18, Mama." Susan looked at her youngest sister, 9-year-old Nancy, her dangling braids brushing the rag rug where she sat cross-legged beside the fire stringing slices of fresh apple rings on a thread of spun flax. Mukki, the family's aging golden-haired spaniel, was curled up in her usual evening spot beside the youngest child. Susan sighed. "Still, it seems like only yesterday that I snuggled by the hearth just like Nan, except our entire cabin would have nearly fit into this room."

Catherine nodded. "Yes, and our *entire* family, all 12 of us, somehow managed to squeeze inside." She sighed. "Hard to imagine. True, the younger ones didn't take up as much space as they do now, but they certainly kept things lively."

"This grand new kitchen has been my favorite part of the house since Papa added it five years ago," Susan said. "And evening is my favorite time here, with  all of our chores over and the day winding down. My sweet memories of our old small cabin come back to life a bit with us all gathered so close together."

Sitting opposite her older sister, 14-year-old Cate's brown eyes flashed their familiar sparkle. "What I remember missing the most after we moved into this new stone manor was all of the sisters sleeping together in the girls' loft." She held the homespun shirt she was mending at arm's length to inspect the new seam and smiled at Nancy. "Except Nan – she was still in a cradle near Mama and Papa's bed." Nan shrugged slightly as Cate continued. "In our new house my sleeping pallet next to Susan and Rebecca's bed in the upstairs bedroom felt cold and lonely, as if I'd lost half of my family."

An arc of dark ringlets capped 16-year-old Rebecca's forehead as she slowed the spinning wheel and pinched the twisted flax filament between her fingers. "You were usually wedged between Susan and me by morning until the three of us just couldn't fit in the bed anymore."

Catherine squinted at the kitchen window facing the back yard and separate summer kitchen building beyond. "Elizabeth should soon be finished helping with the candle dipping out there. I suspect Mollie's papa is playing some merry tunes on that penny flute of his."

"You're probably right about that," agreed 21-year-old Jacob from the corner of the room. The split log bench where he sat was strewn with straps of the leather harness he was repairing.

Susan sneaked a glance at her brother and frowned to herself. *He can hardly keep from smiling – every time that Mollie's name is mentioned or when she sashays by. All the men do. She's got all their heads spinning.*

Not noticing Susan's disapproving look, Jacob added, "Mollie's papa can play some fine music, but he's also been a *fine* worker at our mill – and since the season's end he hasn't hesitated to help David with the tanning. Some men won't go near the stench, but Ephraim's never once complained."

"It was certainly a stroke of good fortune that the Nulls' mule pulled up lame as they were passing through Waynesburg last May, or they might've kept right on going to Pittsburgh," said Catherine. "I remember how exhausted Mollie and her papa looked that day. They'd been traveling for nearly two weeks from Virginia looking for work after her mama and little brother died in that terrible house fire. They were at their wit's end by the time that mule gave out. Lucky for us, I'd say."

I'm sure all the menfolk around here would agree, Susan thought, looping a strand of yarn a little too tightly over her bone knitting needle.

Jacob kneaded a strap of leather between his fingers in search of thinning areas. "Ephraim's often said that once he got a look at the thriving, well-ordered farmstead, he didn't have to think twice about staying. Guess we forget sometimes how fortunate our family's been."

Catherine's thoughts zipped though a swift 40-year history of their farmstead in the Cumberland Valley just east of Waynesburg, Pennsylvania. From the first hundred or so acres Daniel had purchased from her father in 1779, until now, the Royer's local holdings had grown to nearly 950 acres including a large woodlot in the forested area some miles to the west. She pictured the fields of flax, corn, wheat, numerous vegetables and apple, pear and cherry trees – milk cows, horses, hogs, chickens and so on – the endless meals served to their large family and the hired workers who operated the tannery, gristmill, sawmill and creamery on the property and the many prayers they had offered as part of their German Baptist work ethic of giving daily reverence to the Lord for their blessings.

Ten children and 32 years with my Daniel, she mused. *Our sweet Polly's been with the Lord for over five years and Samuel and John are over the mountain so far away.*

Samuel, 29 and John, 23, had moved many days travel north to Huntingdon County to assist with an iron forge operation co-owned by their father and his brother. Soon after that their sister, Polly, died in childbirth and her widowed husband, George Schmucker, joined his brother-in-laws at the iron works. Catherine closed her eyes and pictured the delicate *Scherenschnitte* snowflake Polly had skillfully cut from parchment paper on the last Valentine's Day she was with them that was tucked safely in the family Bible.

Now, in the fall of 1821, nine Royers remained at home, along with a handful of hired help to keep the wheels of the farmstead turning.

A strong draft of damp evening air flattened the fireplace flames as 27-year-old Elizabeth ducked into the kitchen from the back yard. She pushed the heavy, wooden door shut and loosened her woolen cape to hang on the wall pegs next to her brothers' broad-brimmed black hats. Susan glimpsed the rare glow on her eldest sister's face. *Good to see Elizabeth happy. She's been sad for so long.* In spite of her sister's lighter mood, Susan frowned slightly. *Still, a smile's a smile. Even if Mollie's the one responsible for it.*

Elizabeth smoothed her dark hair on either side of the center part, rubbed her chilled hands briskly together and extended them toward the hearth. The flickering firelight intensified the red flush of her high cheekbones tinged pink by the cold night air. She looked around the room. "I was a little worried that I might have delayed Papa's devotions this evening. The sun's setting so quickly now."

"No matter," answered Catherine tipping her head toward the back office down the front hall. "Your papa and David have been poring over their papers and talking business since we left the supper table, but I suspect we'll be seeing them here soon."

 "Mollie and I finished more than four dozen candles, Mama," Elizabeth reported. "She told her papa that he'd best start using the light of the moon to find his way or she'd have no arms left to fix his meals." She shook her head grinning. "Can't help but laugh when she says such things. She sows happiness wherever she goes." She moved to the bench beside Jacob and murmured, "Like Polly – so much like . . ."

By nature the most quiet and reverent of the siblings, Elizabeth, more than anyone, missed the high spirits of her late sister and soulmate, Polly. Born just two years apart, they had shared a special bond that had balanced and nourished them both. The void had been slow to fill until Mollie Null arrived.

Susan didn't share Elizabeth's fondness for the new arrival. Having heard more than she wanted about Mollie, she set her needle and thread aside and rubbed her eyes. "Hope Papa comes soon. I can hardly keep awake enough to stitch up this sock properly."

"Well, you need wait no longer, *Tochter*," came a deep rumble from beyond the room. Daniel's sturdy frame filled the doorway to the adjacent dining room. The large family Bible rested in the crook of his arm. David, the eldest, moved in behind him and shifted a heavy oak chair next to his mother, establishing the hub of the circle for the head of the family. Fatigue ringed both men's eyes.

Daniel stepped to his seat barely disguising the catch in his stride aggravated by a sore hip. His broad, but aging shoulders rounded into a hump as he bent his head over the heavy tome in his lap. David dropped onto the bench on the other side of Jacob.

Opening the Bible across his lap, Daniel scanned the room to confirm all were present. As each folded their hands, he began, "This evening's reading will be *Psalm 128* to remind us of the bounty the Lord has granted our family.

"Blessed is every one that feareth the Lord; that walketh
in His ways. For thou shalt eat the labour of thine
hands: happy shalt thou be, and it shall be well with thee . . ."

After the prayer and communal *Amen*, Susan was the first to rise. "Guess I'll lead the way to bed tonight." She yawned and rotated her head to ease her aching neck – and to send Rebecca a not-so-subtle sidelong glance inviting her to retire early as well.

Rebecca caught Susan's meaning and tied off the flaxen thread of the spinning wheel as she yawned deeply. "I won't be far behind, *Schwester*."

"Me either," added Cate, well attuned to the undercurrent between her sisters that escaped the rest of the family. "Wouldn't want to wake you two by coming into the room later. Besides, all that yawning's made me sleepy, too." As she followed her sisters toward the stairway in the front hall, she handed Jacob the mended shirt. "Be sure you get enough rest to keep your eyes open at the mill. A shirtsleeve is much simpler to fix than a broken arm."

"*Danke, Schwester*," he said laying the garment beside him. "I'll try to be more careful from now on."

Cate checked the upstairs hall to make sure no one had followed them and then closed the bedroom door behind her. Susan and Rebecca were already sitting together on the bed whispering.

"What's going on?" she asked as she knelt between them on the floor.

"Mollie Null's 'going on,'" Susan grumped. "And I intend to stop her."

"What do you mean, 'going on?'" asked Cate.

"She means that she's tired of the way Mollie has the men around here 'going on' whenever she's around – especially Henry Reighart," Rebecca huffed.

Susan jabbed Rebecca with her elbow. "Not just me – and not just Henry, either," she snapped. "Those tight bodices and the skirts she wears nearly up to her knees have the whole town talking."

"So what are you planning to do, Susan?" said Cate grinning with anticipation.

"Not just *me* – *us*," Susan said drawing her sisters closer and lowering her voice as if someone might overhear, even through the closed door. "Every Saturday Market Day this harvest, I've noticed that Mollie disappears for at least an hour around midday. And when she shows up later, her cheeks are flushed and she keeps smiling to herself."

"Really?" Cate's eyes widened.

"Really!" Rebecca echoed. "*And* Susan and I noticed last Saturday that Henry Reighart goes missing at the same time – and acts all nervous when he shows up again."

"So," Susan continued, "this Saturday, between the three of us, we'll find out exactly where Mollie's been going. Not a word to anybody 'til we know just what we're talking about." She nodded to Cate and Rebecca in turn. "Agreed?"

They nodded back.

In the kitchen, Elizabeth rose from her seat beside Jacob. She settled into the chair next to her mother that her father had vacated after devotions to complete some final figures in his office before retiring for the night. "Mama, do you think it would be fitting to offer to make Mollie a new dress?"

Catherine anchored her needle into her embroidery and considered. "As I recall, there's a sizeable piece of homespun under my bed. Most of you children have stopped outgrowing your clothes from one season to the next, so I have some extra. Now that you mention it, her clothes are a little worn. With the harvest and preserving, I hadn't noticed what she was wearing."

"Mollie's grown a little since she came here," said Elizabeth lowering her eyes.

"*Ja*," said Catherine. "Mollie's taken a real liking to our cooking. Good to see some more meat on that poor girl's bones. I'm sure we could find the time to fashion something for her. Must be mindful, though, not to imply that the clothes she has now aren't sufficient and embarrass her or her father."

"I know, Mama. But folks are talking about how immodest she is because she's outgrown her bodice and shows too much of her ankle. They don't consider that she hasn't got a mama to help her with such things. I think I could make the offer and not offend her, if you approve."

Catherine wrapped her arm around Elizabeth's shoulder and drew her near. "You're a fine daughter for thinking so kindly of your friend. We'll get started on that dress as soon as Mollie's ready."

"Danke, Mutter." Elizabeth returned the hug.

"Bitte, Tochter." Catherine cooed. "Time we all got to bed." She looked toward Jacob and David both finishing up the leather work. "Last one to bed banks the fire."

"Yes, Mama," Jacob answered for them both.

Elizabeth nudged a drowsy Nan and led her gently toward their upstairs bedroom. Mukki, her muzzle streaked with silver, stretched out by the fire as the last of the Royers made an end to their day.

-2-

To Town on Market Day

"Plant yourself right here, Nan," said Mollie patting a space on the wagon bed between herself and Elizabeth. "Wouldn't want to be late for Market Day." Mollie's wavy golden hair trailed down her back and in front of her shoulders curling against her tanned neck and collarbones above the gathered bodice of her rough, homespun dress. David and Jacob sat on the other side facing them. Her crystal-blue eyes sparked at Jacob when she caught sight of his approving glance.

"*Danke*, Mollie," said Nan scurrying to get settled. "Ready, Papa," she called to Daniel seated beside Catherine on the wagon seat.

"Is this all that's going, *meine Frau?*" he asked Catherine noticing more empty space in the wagon bed than was usual for a family outing.

"*Ja, mein Mann*. The other girls were late getting to their chores today. They asked if they could bring the buggy into town later and I agreed rather than make the rest of us late. *Ist gut?*"

"Nein," he groused. "Have to do for now, but next time they can either be ready or stay at home. We're not in the business of wearing out another horse."

Catherine sighed. "Only two more Saturday Markets left this season. I'll let them know your feelings on it. They enjoy going, so I'm sure they won't be late again." She patted the dark bun streaked with gray at the base of her white cap, pulled on the loops of the bow to her modesty cape and rose slightly to adjust the folds of her long skirt under her ample hips.

Daniel pressed on the top of his broad brimmed hat, pushed his salt and pepper beard back against his collarless shirt and flicked the reins. Siggy, the sturdy old family mule, started with a lurch.

"Why the long face, David?" asked Mollie staring at him as they bumped along the well-worn dirt road to town. She lifted her arms and embraced the sky. "It's a beautiful day for some fun. The leaves are gettin' their fall blush and the sun and blue sky are nearly perfect."

Jacob drank in her glee and patted David's shoulder. "David's idea of fun is having all the figures balance at the end of the day – in *our* favor. I think going to Market Day is his Saturday chore. Right, *Bruder?*"

"Can't afford to miss the conversations – the information. Too many decisions we have to make depend on what's happening in town. Competition for the mill and hides and such is getting tougher every day," David grumbled.

"Well, I don't want to miss the brown sugar candy," said Nan. "It's so sweet it makes my teeth hurt – but in a good way."

"If it's all been sold, I'm sure *Frau* Frantz will still have some tasty ginger snaps or apple dumplings at her stand. She must work day and night on Fridays to have such a store of good things to sell," said Elizabeth.

"Well, we're soon there," said Daniel as they passed the tollgate just east of the town limits. The stile had been raised and no tolls were being collected so as not to discourage any and all from joining in the town's festivities.

Catherine looked back into the wagon. "Make sure to be just south of the town pump by the time the pump's shadow touches the east end of the square in front of Stoner's Tavern."

"It's a long, and probably dark, walk home if you're late," Daniel warned.

"Whew!" said Rebecca dumping the last of the fireplace ashes into the leaching barrel beside the smokehouse. "Never worked so hard at *not* working before."

Susan came out of the barn leading Maggie hitched to the small, black buggy. Cate was already seated inside giddy with the prospect of carrying out their plan. "I think we all three did a fine job of slowing down without anyone noticing, don't you, Susan?"

Rebecca brushed the flakes of ash from her skirt as she hopped up beside her sister. "But that was the easy part, wasn't it, Susan?"

Susan remained silent as she shifted the reins back over Maggie's mane and took her seat beside them. "Yes and yes," she said looking at Cate and then Rebecca respectively. "Now we have our own transportation and much more opportunity to wander where we need to without causing suspicion. Next thing is to get Maggie moving before Mollie has such a head start that we can't follow her."

After wending his way through the milling crowds and vendors gathered around the heart of Waynesburg's large main square, Daniel turned left and drew back Elsie's reins stopping at the large hitching post just south of Hiram Hennberger's candy store.

Jacob was the first to jump out of the wagon. Nan scurried to where he stood and leapt from the wagon bed into his waiting arms. "I spied Hannah Baer over by Mrs. Frantz's stand, Mama," she squealed dashing to the front of the wagon to hurry her mother along. "With all of those 13 brothers and sisters in her family, the sweets could be gone before we get there."

"Be calm, *Liebling*," Catherine urged as Daniel helped her to the ground. "More than pastries and sugar candy to be considered. I noticed some fine fabrics by the weaver's display and Mr. Bell's pottery wares are not to be missed."

Mollie was the next one out of the wagon much to Jacob's liking as he took her hand to steady her exit. She batted her eyelashes and affected the air of a fine lady as he helped her. "Thank you kindly, sir," she said, color warming her cheeks.

Jacob felt his face flush, but before he could respond, Mollie was off at nearly a run waving back at them. "Got some errands I must do for Da. I'll meet all of you as soon as I can." Then she disappeared around the corner and back up Main Street.

Elizabeth frowned a bit watching her vanish. "Wonder where she's off to again? Seems like every Market Day gets her so wound up that I can't keep up with her."

"She's just got lots of spirit," Jacob explained staring at the path Mollie had just left behind her.

"David!" barked Daniel. "That's Patrick Mooney over by the White Swan. Good time to ask him what he thinks about everyone's claims on the creek lately. The Antietam serves us well and we'd best preserve that advantage."

"*Ja, Vater*," David answered. "And Jacob should come, as well. The mill's worthless without waterpower." He turned to his brother and whispered. "Best you get your mind off women and on waterwheels and grinding stones."

"And best you not be judging my thoughts, *Bruder*," Jacob answered with an irritation contrary to his nature. David's gruffness rarely bothered him, but lately he had become more defensive if Mollie was in any way involved.

"Enough," said Daniel. "We've business to attend to."

Catherine and Elizabeth shook their heads as the men moved off and Nan tugged impatiently on her mother's arm. Elizabeth wondered aloud, "Jacob appears to be *taken* with Mollie." She looked at Catherine. "How do you feel about that, *Mutter*?"

"That's a difficult matter. Though Mollie's not of our fellowship of believers, she's a good, sweet tempered young woman devoted to her father and not afraid of hard work." Lost momentarily in considering the rest of her response, she was oblivious to Nan's persistent pulling. "But, Jacob needs and deserves a loving companion to share his life, and the Lord makes such things happen as He will." She fought to suppress a smile. "I suppose we shall see. Now, let's get this child to *Frau* Frantz's before I lose my arm."

Elizabeth snatched Nan away from her mother's hand. She crossed her arms and peered wide-eyed at her little sister. "Last one to the sweets stand empties all the chamber pots tomorrow." In a twitter of giggles, they dashed off.

Maggie's clip-clops beat a rapid pace kicking up puffs of dust as Susan clicked her tongue in encouragement. The three sisters, intent on their mission, leaned forward in the small, black buggy's enclosure. "Start looking for Mollie and Henry as soon as we get close to town," said Susan. "We have a lot of ground to cover and the crowds may be pretty thick by now. Hard to miss Mollie's blond hair the way it's always flying and Henry's taller than most," Susan instructed.

"And more handsome," said Cate.

"If *you* say so," Susan replied.

"Oh, I think you *know* so, truth be told," teased Rebecca.

"Hush, both of you," said Susan. "The tollgate is just ahead. Shut your mouths and open your eyes."

Craning her head to take in the small log school house on the rise just behind the tollgate, Cate remarked, "I suppose you won't miss Rebecca and me when we start back to school soon."

"I'll certainly welcome the quiet," Susan admitted. "Between you and . . ."

"Wait!" Cate yelped. "There she is!"

Susan and Rebecca turned to her as Maggie continued her gait. Cate reached across Susan and yanked the reins jerking the horse's head sharply. "Mollie!" she explained to their confused faces. "I just saw Mollie on Burns Hill, behind the schoolhouse. She's probably over the top by now the way she's moving."

Susan and Rebecca followed Cate's stare to the steep, grassy knoll to their right, but saw nothing.

18

"Are you sure?" Susan asked squinting.

"I know what I saw," said Cate.

"We can't take a chance," said Susan. "Rebecca, I'll pull up just past the tollgate and let you out. Do the best you can to follow her without being seen. I need to get the buggy to town and find Henry. Cate's eagle eyes will help me more than you right now."

As the buggy slowed, Rebecca hopped out, but hesitated a moment. "I hope Mollie stays clear of the graveyard up there. I hate graveyards."

"Just do the best you can and meet us in town later when you know something. Don't be so long that anyone gets suspicious." Rebecca nodded. "Godspeed," Susan said and snapped the reins as Rebecca scurried up the hill.

"Not much to buy or many folks to see on the other side of that hill," Susan shared with Cate as the buggy rattled on towards town.

"But a mighty good place to be out of sight and still be close to town," Cate added to the stew.

"Exactly what I was thinking, *Schwester*."

"And look!" Cate said pointing to the side of the road just ahead of the buggy. "What do you think about this fine figure of a man taking a stroll toward the Burns Hill graveyard path?"

"Henry Reighart!" Susan's eyes popped as she cursed herself for saying the name so loudly.

Henry had been chewing on a strand of beef jerky and studying the scattered stones and dust he scuffed at as he ambled along. Tall and lanky, a fringe of wheat-colored locks curtained his forehead under his black hat. Hearing his name, he looked up, his hazel eyes freezing at the sight of Susan and Cate. He quickly summoned a strained smile on his high-cheek boned face and waved. "Uh, hello, ladies. You're a little late getting to town, aren't you?"

"A little," Susan admitted. "And you're a little early *leaving* Market Day, aren't *you*?"

"Just needed to get away from the crowds," Henry said unconvincingly. "Thought I might climb up Burns Hill and get a bird's-eye view of the town."

"Well," Susan said with a stiff grin, "that sounds like a grand idea. Maybe I'll let Cate take the buggy on in to town and join you."

Henry looked at the ground. "I . . . uh . . . I mean, you . . . You might miss the best of the offerings in town if you stop here first."

"Can't think of a thing I need more than a look at the view you just mentioned. Besides, I'm saving up for the last Market Day of the season when the prices drop." Susan handed Cate the reins and got out as a knowing look passed between them.

Without hesitation, Cate shook the reins and left Henry with no choice but to deal with Susan.

No sooner had Susan's feet hit the ground than she tromped off in the direction where Rebecca had seen Mollie head earlier. When Henry failed to follow her, she called back to him over her shoulder. "You mean to tell me that a strapping fellow like yourself can't keep up with a mere girl like me?"

"Susan, wait. You . . ."

"Wait? Why should I *wait* when the day's already late enough?" By now she was nearly halfway up the hill with Henry in pursuit.

"You don't understand, Susan. If you keep . . ."

She turned and glared at him. "Are you trying to say that *if* I keep going, I might see more than a 'bird's-eye view' of town?"

Henry pleaded. "Susan, you don't understand. I was . . ."

"Oh, but I *do* understand – more than you know." She took a few steps down the hill toward him. "You see, I *saw* Mollie run up over this same hill just a few minutes ago – this hill that you're about to climb to get a look at 'the town.' Maybe the town *flirt* is more like it!" She pivoted and did her best to jog ahead enough to get a glimpse of the other side of the hill.

"But, Susan . . . ," Henry insisted. "It's not *me* who wants to look." He reached out to grab her arm, but missed and lost his footing. As he broke his fall and rolled over, he yelled, though he knew it was futile, "Susan, don't!"

As his warning echoed behind her, she stopped in her tracks. Scurrying down the other side of the hill, darting between the small, scattered headstones were Mollie and a formidable young man. Susan squinted hard, but couldn't identify Mollie's companion. She huffed and crossed her arms over her chest, but suddenly realized what was most important. *It's not Henry who's running away!*

She slowly turned and saw Henry sitting on the ground shaking his head with his palms upturned in front of him as if to say, 'I told you not to go.' Now she wished *she* could disappear, just like Mollie. She prayed for one of the graves to open up and swallow her. She felt her face redden. *What have I done? – and, Oh, no! Where's Rebecca?*

Henry looked at her with a sad smile, extended his hand. "Since I'm no longer needed as a lookout, would you care to accompany me to town?"

Susan nodded and then started to shuffle in his direction with her head down.

"Just one thing," Henry said as she took his hand to help him up off the ground, "Don't ask me who you just saw with Mollie. That's a secret I mean to keep."

Both Susan and Henry knew that he was quite able to help himself up, but they welcomed the excuse for the brief contact. As they tightened their grip on each other's hand, Susan felt her stomach flutter and Henry's heart raced a little faster.

They paused for a long second before relinquishing their grasp. She squared her shoulders and looked toward town. "It's a fine day for market, isn't it?"

"It is that," he agreed.

-3-

Trouble at the Mill

The heavy air of a late afternoon hung on the rolling hills of the Blue Ridge Mountains and cast an oppression of spent energy across the Royer farmstead. Everyone had been working at their various tasks since they had risen to their breakfast of cornmeal mush and molasses hours before, stopping only for noon meal. Jacob Royer and Ephraim Null's clothes had grown pale under the coating of the fine airborne powder of the gristmill as the massive, precisely balanced millstones pulverized load after load of rye grain.

Despite the October chill, Jacob had worked up a sweat. His forehead looked like a whitewashed fence where he had brushed it with his hand. He glanced upward at Ephraim who was checking on the teeth of the wooden gears and condition of the large grinding millstones on the balcony nearly 10 feet above. *Don't know what I*

did without Ephraim, Jacob thought. *As smart as he is strong. Not many can learn to read the stones and gears so quickly and still be willing and able to do hard labor.* He cinched shut the newly filled sack. *And he produced a fine, sweet daughter.* Jacob shut his eyes for a brief second to picture Mollie's smile.

"Millstones look good. Should be fine flour again this run," Ephraim shouted down to Jacob over the roar of the grinding from his second-story perch high in the bowels of the cavernous building. Outside, the waterfall from the mill pond fed by the Antietam Creek pushed the gigantic wooden waterwheel to its optimum speed in this busy harvest season. "No surprise," Ephraim continued, "with the high quality grain from such well managed fields. Farms around here always look as if they're groomed for a Saturday night in town."

"Or a Sunday Meeting," Jacob replied raising a fog as he tossed a 40-pound sack of rye flour on top of a growing pile.

Ephraim paused in his duties and pulled out the silver locket he always kept in his waist pocket. "My wife, God rest her soul, would be pleased at your correction," he hollered. "Never could get me to church as much as she would've liked." He raised the treasure to his lips, but the burnished silver heart slipped between his fingers. Lunging to retrieve it, he stumbled and his rear foot slipped off the wood-planked work platform toward the rotating cogs. Ephraim scrambled frantically, but the other leg lost its grip as well and went over the edge leaving the desperate man clinging to the second story floorboards by his clenched fingers.

Jacob watched in horror from below as Ephraim dangled dangerously close to the maw of the machinery. "Ephraim!" he yelled. "Hang on. I'll stop the wheel." He shot out the side door toward the wooden sluice gates that controlled the flow of water diverted from the mill pond to the large wheel that powered the massive gears.

"Hurry, Jacob!" Ephraim screamed. "Hurry!"

Jacob's chest pulsated into his throat as he struggled against the moisture-swollen levers. *Gott im Himmel, give me strength*, he prayed. *Help me. Help me save Ephraim.*

Looking away from his tenuous hold to the threatening scene below, Ephraim's heart froze. The teeth of the rotating gears were licking the torn cuff of his trousers. Despair seized him when he felt a distinct tug followed by a sustained pull as the 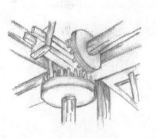 mechanism began to devour the heavy fabric that strangled his leg. Quickly his body was stretched to the limit and the critical curl of his fingers began to straighten.

Even above his loud shouts of protest – "No . . . ! God Almighty, no . . . ! Ephraim heard the snap and crunch of the bones of

25

his leg being crushed by the machine's indifferent jaws. The delay between the moment of injury and the sensation of pain was a purgatory of disbelief. "Dear God, not my leg!" he pleaded with an irrational hope of altering the inevitable.

The lurid splash of red blood on the rough gray millstone as it ground to a slow halt confirmed the ghastly truth. Like a river of fire, an excruciating pain suddenly flooded his leg and chest. His shrieks echoed in the mill rafters and then faded as his body went limp. It fell with a dull thud against the side of the finally stilled gear that held Ephraim's body in its talons like a hawk.

He remained blessedly unconscious as Jacob and David struggled to release what was left of his leg. With the help of other workers alerted by the shrieks, the two Royer brothers carried Ephraim's mangled, bleeding body to the sleeping pallet in the summer kitchen.

Unaware of the gruesome drama unfolding on the far side of the property, Susan and Rebecca straddled their three-legged milking stools as the spurts of milk they squeezed from the dairy cows' udders stung the sides of their oak buckets. "Well, all we know is that he looked as strong as an ox and has a mane of black hair," said Susan. "And I dare not ask Henry any more. As it is, he was especially kind not to tease me about what happened."

"And what'll we say to Mollie *today*? The way she looked at us in the wagon on the way back home yesterday said everything. She obviously saw us following her. Thank goodness she didn't tell the others," said Rebecca. "What if she . . .?"

"Hush!" warned Susan looking beyond Rebecca's shoulder toward the opening door.

"What if she tells people that Susan and Rebecca Royer hide in the bushes and spy on things that are none of their concern?" fired Mollie, her eyes flashing as she stomped into the barn and completed Rebecca's sentence. "What if she . . . ," but her voice faltered. She crumpled onto a scatter of hay, covered her face and began to cry.

Clearly perplexed by Mollie's tears, Susan looked at Rebecca and indicated with a nod of her head toward the house that Rebecca should leave the two of them alone. Rebecca understood immediately. She rose, grabbed both milk buckets and slipped out.

As the barn door slammed behind her, Susan lowered herself beside Mollie and waited for her to speak. Mollie sniffled loudly a few times, and then drew a deep breath as she wiped her eyes with the backs of her hands. "I know that looked just awful yesterday – me sneaking around with a fella in the graveyard and all." Her shoulders jerked as the words caught in her throat. "But Jacob . . . "

Jacob? Susan was shocked at the mention of her brother's name, but remained silent as Mollie continued, "Jacob's so sweet. I don't mean to hurt him, but . . . I can tell he likes me a bit . . . and I really like him, too. He's a fine, decent man . . . Da respects him so much, but . . . ." Mollie laid her head on her crossed arms resting on her knees and sobbed.

Susan wrapped her arm around Mollie's shoulder. "I'm so sorry, Mollie. I was wrong to spy on you that way. It's just that I was . . . I was worried that my Henry Reighart . . . I mean, that Henry Reighart was taken with you."

Mollie looked at her dumbfounded. "Henry?"

Susan shook her head. "It was silly jealousy that made me do such a shameful thing – and I even got Rebecca and Cate to help me." She squeezed Mollie. "Please forgive me."

"Oh, Susan, the whole county knows how much Henry Reighart cares for you. He would never look at another girl that way." Susan blushed as Mollie continued, "Seems like we all do crazy things when these menfolk get inside our heads. I just wish that . . ."

Just then, Jacob burst through the door in a panic and swept the saddle from its place by the stall. He caught sight of the girls on the floor and froze. Blood was splattered across his sleeves and chest and streaked his stricken face. "*Mein Gott,*" he said as he dropped the tack and knelt in front of them. "There's been a horrible accident – at the mill." He took Mollie's hands. "Your papa, Mollie, he's . . . I've got to get Doctor Bonebreak, right now!"

Mollie and Susan jumped up in alarm. "Da? Where's Da?" Mollie screamed as Susan stood at the ready to support her.

"We got him free of the gears, Mollie. He's in the summer kitchen." Mollie bolted for the door, Jacob calling after her, "Mama and Elizabeth are with him." He caught Susan by the arm as she started to run after Mollie. "Take care of my Mollie, Susan. Her papa's bad – really bad. I doubt he'll make it."

As Jacob galloped toward Waynesburg, the grisly scene moments before at the mill spun in his head. He spurred Maggie and leaned low and forward in the saddle. *Hang on, Ephraim. Such a good man.* Swirling clouds of dust hung behind him as he dodged early morning travelers on the main road to town. "Go, Maggie," he urged and bit his lower lip. *Poor Mollie. What'll she do without her father, if . . . ?*

Horse and rider flew past the tollgate. *My Mollie – Why did I say 'my Mollie' to Susan? God knows that's what I want, but . . .* "God help us all. Faster, Maggie," he pleaded. Even as he fought to manage Maggie's unrestrained gallop, he shivered at the recent memory. He pulled the reins hard toward him drawing Maggie's head back almost to his lap when they reached Doctor Bonebreak's house. Tossing the leather straps aside he leapt from the saddle, raced up the front steps and pounded on the door. *"Herr Doktor! Herr Doktor! Kommen Sie schnell!"*

29

The Fabric of Life

Doctor Bonebreak stood solemnly under the low eave in the corner of the small, one-room summer kitchen. Just moments after his arrival, he had determined that no skill he possessed could save poor Ephraim. He'd lost too much blood and his broken body was in shock. The best any physician could offer was a draft of laudanum to alleviate whatever pain Catherine's mixture of warm milk and crushed poppy seeds couldn't.

Subdued agony and grief thickened the air. The doctor drew shallow breaths, lowered his head and waited in deference to the tortured mourners who surrounded Ephraim in his final moments in this life. *Death always smells the same*, thought Dr. Bonebreak watching the tableau. *The foul odor of defeated life smothers everything it touches, until the merciful end finally comes.* Catherine joined him, knowing as well that she could do no more than offer prayers and wait to comfort the grieving.

Mollie's rumpled blond hair fell across the brown woolen blanket that covered her father. She knelt beside him and cradled his cool, pale hand in her own trying to warm it – revive it – as she pressed it against her warm cheek. Dark uneven streaks drawn by earlier tears etched her face with unspoken fear.

The wavering figures hovering nearby puzzled Ephraim as his eyes fluttered open. They were beside him, yet beyond. *Jacob and*

30

Elizabeth? Why are they . . . ? Mollie's whimpering drew his glance to her head resting ever so lightly on his chest. She was holding his hand – he could see that. *Strange, I can't feel it,* he thought. "Mollie?" he mouthed, but he didn't hear his voice. "Mollie?" he tried again with more deliberate effort.

As his daughter anxiously lifted her tear-filled eyes to his, Ephraim suddenly understood everything. *I'm dying,* he considered with untroubled certainty. *It's my time.*

"Da! Oh, Da, can you hear me?" Mollie urged inching closer to his face. His slight smile confirmed that he was still with her, but the peace in his expression, no longer contorted by pain, both calmed and frightened her.

The dying man raised his chin ever so slightly toward Jacob and Elizabeth who leaned in at the subtle but clear invitation. "Jacob – Elizabeth, take care of my Mollie. Don't let her be alone after . . ."

Mollie's sobs drowned the rest of his request, but Jacob and Elizabeth both nodded. Elizabeth knelt beside Mollie in prayer and Jacob gently laid his hands on their shoulders.

Again, Ephraim managed the shadow of a smile. He returned to his distraught daughter. "Mollie . . . Mollie . . . ?" Jacob squeezed her shoulder to alert her to Ephraim's call. As her eyes begged her dear father to stay, he left her with his dying request. "Be happy, Mollie, my girl. Be happy."

-4-

Corn Shucks and Kisses

"Looks like half the county's here," said George Smith as he leaned his massive shoulder against the stout support beam of the Reigharts' barn. He stared beyond Henry's head at the covey of older girls buzzing about the annual shucking competition to come. They were speculating about which of the many anxious young men milling around the property would find the one corn cob dyed red and hidden in the huge pile of unshucked ears that filled the center of the barn. The winner could kiss his choice of eligible young ladies.

The Royers and their neighbors managed to combine most of the monumental tasks of farm life with fun and fellowship. Everyone knew corn was an essential staple. *What would we do without cornmeal for cooking, winter fodder for the livestock, sweet corn syrup from the hard-boiled cobs and more?* thought George, studying the mound. *The more hands the better for all the harvesting and shucking.*

The Royers of Renfrew

This mid-afternoon October Saturday was crisp and ripe, humming with conversations and laughter. Most folks had already spent plenty of energy on chores at their own homes before the gathering. But the steaming dishes and heavily laden baskets resting on long makeshift tables drew the playful enthusiasm of scurrying children. The autumn glow of the deep amber sun across the valley sparked a new rush of excitement.

Henry walked over to his friend and slapped his upper arm. "George, if you were pointing a rifle, I'd swear we'd have fresh venison for supper," he said. "Want to give me a hint about what – or *who* – you're tracking here today?"

George grinned with a sidelong glance at his friend. "Actually, I'm takin' in a part of your hunting grounds, I'd say."

"What?" Henry drew back.

"The Royer acres," George explained. "They sure grow some fine young ladies. Susan's already in *your* sights, but *I'm* feeling mighty partial to her curly haired younger sister."

"Rebecca?" Henry ventured.

"If that's her name – the one standing right behind Susan – then I'm thinking you need to introduce us."

Henry checked quickly to confirm his guess and then shook his head at George. "That's Rebecca all right," he said. "But you might want to think twice. She's feistier than a wet hen, that one."

"Maybe that's what puts the sparkle in those brown eyes," George joked. "I've handled many a strong, stubborn mule in my time. That sweet girl doesn't scare me."

"Neither did that huge gelding that smashed your leg and left you limping," Henry warned.

George rubbed his right knee. "Doesn't slow me down much, and the catch in my step gains me some sympathy and attention from the ladies. That mule may actually have done me a favor. Can't say I really miss wrestling those high-strung Goliaths down muddy timber trails at the iron works. And this bum leg couldn't keep up with you masons mixing and hauling all of that mortar and stone."

"I know the forge workers have been thankin' that mule, too," said Henry. "Since you started managing the company store, the scrip they get paid in goes a lot further than before."

"I do what I can. Lord knows, it's hardly enough, but what can *you* do for me *now* as far as Miss Rebecca is concerned?" asked George.

"Well, the shucking contest is starting in just a few minutes. After that's over and the business of winnin' and kissin' is past, she'll be less distracted and maybe a bit more willing to pay you some mind."

"You just make the introductions, Brother." George swelled his chest and straightened his newfangled suspender straps over the front of his plain cut shirt. "I'll handle it from there, First, I intend to find that red ear of corn and beat you to those comely Royer sisters."

34

"Let's sit over there," said Elizabeth indicating to Mollie two upturned apple baskets near the double door of the barn.

"Is that close enough to see everything?" asked Mollie. "I know you've been to this event every year, but I've never seen it before."

"It's the same place Polly and I used to sit. She used to say that it was better than getting lost in the crowd that pushes in so close." *Good to see Mollie smiling*, thought Elizabeth. *Getting some of her old spirit back.*

"From what you've told me about Polly," said Mollie, "I trust whatever advice she gave you." Mollie drew back her shoulders and smoothed the skirt of the new dress Catherine had made for her, by far a more modest version of the worn frock it replaced, but still a fair complement to her fine figure. A more demur bun now held her long, blond hair at the nape of her neck, but this change gave full play to her translucent blue eyes.

As they took their seats, *Herr* Reighart planted himself at the head of the towering mountain of corn and shouted to the crowd. "Last call for those fellows game enough to make quick work of these husks. Keep a sharp eye out for that special red cob."

In seconds all the available young ladies encircled the mound allowing just enough room for the inner circle of young men eager for the starting bell.

Jacob Royer dashed around the corner of the door and stopped in front of Elizabeth and Mollie. "*Gut.* I'm not too late," he panted. "I haven't been a part of this since my older brothers came to blows over the outcome nearly ten years ago. Since then, I've never really had a good reason for winning . . ." He gazed at Mollie. ". . .'til now."

Mollie bowed her head slightly and returned his smile. As Jacob joined the other men, Elizabeth gave Mollie a gentle nudge with her elbow and Mollie shrugged shyly.

The bell sounded and the melee began. Amid the shower of dried husks and billowy cornsilk, Elizabeth paused to study Mollie's reaction to this *new* event. *Odd,* she thought as she watched Mollie follow Jacob's progress, *the spark's gone. She's more content than happy, now. Not as excited as she was earlier. I wonder . . ."*

The brittle stack melted away like a snowball in August as a dozen or more pairs of calloused and scored hands ripped the dried covering from the plump kerneled cobs. The odds of discovering the fought-after prize were improving by the second. Suddenly a victory shout brought the frenzy to a halt.

"I've got it!" Waving the evidence high above his head, Henry Reighart emerged from the rubble of discarded fodder. All eyes, including Henry's, turned immediately in Susan's direction. Her cheeks flushed at the rush of attention as she braced herself for Henry's all too public request.

But after taking a step in her direction, Henry veered to the left and began a slow attentive inspection of the other nearby girls. "Afternoon, Ruthie . . . Nice to see you, Charlotte . . . Having fun, Leah?" he kindly offered as he made his way closer to Susan.

As the giggled responses grew, so did the hard line of Susan's mouth. *How dare him!* she fumed to herself. *Why, I'll show him. I'll . . . I'll . . .*

"What's he doing?" Rebecca whispered in Susan's ear.

"How would I know?" she blurted back. "And why should I care?" She fought hard to avoid giving Henry a scowl as she stomped away, but before she could escape, she collided with George Smith who jumped into her path.

"Oh, excuse me, is it Susan?" George apologized.

"Yes, now if you'll kindly get out of my way . . ."

"I'd truly like to do that, but my friend Henry would never forgive me if I did." George looked behind her and yelled. "Now would you, Henry?"

"Never!" proclaimed Henry as he moved up and peeked over Susan's shoulder. "She's the finest prize here – at least in my eyes. And best no one say otherwise."

George made way for Henry to move in and face Susan who was trying desperately not to weaken. "I've come to claim my reward, dear lady, though I know I don't deserve it," said Henry.

"You surely don't," she grumbled.

"But the rules of the game are clear, aren't they?" added George to the spectators approval as they shook their heads and murmured their assent.'

"How fortunate for me," Henry said. "Because I know a girl as virtuous and upright as Susan Royer would not want to break the rules." He bent down to meet her eye to eye. "Would you do me the honor of allowing me to kiss your fair cheek, *mein liebes Mädchen*?"

Oh, you'll pay for this, Henry Reighart! thought Susan as, in spite of her best efforts, she relented and turned her cheek to him. When he kissed it, everyone cheered. Then Henry offered Susan his arm and they walked out the door together followed by the rest of the guests toward the waiting meal. *But you do make me smile, Henry,* Susan mused. *That happiness I can never deny.*

George Smith held his place instead of falling in line with the others heading for the roasted pork, chicken and dumplings, hot cabbage slaw, warm cornbread, apple pandowdy and more. As he had hoped, Rebecca promptly marched over to him, planted her hands on her hips and stared at him hard. "And just where did Henry Reighart find a friend the likes of you, sir? One who would help him pull such a trick."

"George Smith's the name, Miss . . . uh . . . I didn't catch yours," said George tipping his head with an air of innocence.

"Rebecca Royer," she answered making no gesture in response. "Susan's sister. You know, the girl you just helped to embarrass in front of all creation."

George shrugged and shook off Rebecca's subtle snub. "It was meant in fun, *Fräulein* Royer. No harm intended. Had I known you were her sister, I might've reconsidered rather than risk offense. Henry's known for his fine sense of humor, you know."

"And how do you know Henry Reighart, *Herr* Smith?'

"Please, call me George. I met Henry when . . ."

Suddenly a resounding howl and crash directly behind George stopped him mid-sentence as a body fell backwards, spread-eagle from the upper hayloft into the pile of discarded corn shucks.

"Israel Baer, you could've killed yourself, you young fool," scolded Henry's father. "Now get yourself under control and off to dinner."

"Sorry, *Herr* Reighart." Israel scrambled to his feet and lowered his head. A mass of thick, black hair fell forward covering the suppressed pleasure on his face as he feigned contrition. "I just couldn't resist." He drew a deep breath. "I'll probably be just as tempted by that fine food I smell." He looked over at George and Rebecca having narrowly missed them in his descent. He bowed slightly and waved them toward the door. "After you two. Hope I didn't startle you too much."

"We're just fine, but my stomach *has* been wondering if I slit my throat," said George offering his arm to Rebecca.

She pursed her mouth and made her way around him toward Elizabeth and Mollie. She glanced back at George and Israel. "Oh, and while you two are filling your plates, I hope you both help yourselves to an ample serving of good sense, too."

Jacob reached Elizabeth and Mollie just as Rebecca joined them. He shook his head. "That Israel," he said. "He's more than a little *ferhoodled* at times. And that reminds me," he said turning toward Mollie, "Papa told me yesterday that Israel's coming to work at the mill to help with the harvest. That should keep things lively."

Mollie stiffened. "Oh, Jacob. He's so wild. Won't that be too dangerous at the mill with all the gears and . . ." Her voice cracked. "What if something awful happens? What if . . .?"

Jacob immediately regretted what he had said, the horror of the recent accident coming back. *Should know better than to mention the mill*, he told himself. He put his arm gently around Mollie's shoulders. "So sorry, Mollie. I wasn't thinking. Nothing terrible's going to happen. The more hands, the safer and easier the task. You'll see."

Still Mollie's panic persisted. Elizabeth whispered in her ear. "Jacob's right, Mollie. But we'll say an extra prayer for their safety every day."

"Don't be glum, Mollie," chimed Rebecca. She snagged Mollie's hand and dragged her toward the food line. "Just imagine Mrs. Frantz's shoo fly pie meltin' in your mouth and the warm, sweet cider slidin' down your throat." She grabbed Elizabeth with her other hand. "Come on, everybody. Now – before those victuals take a chill!" *And before George Smith catches up*, she added to herself as she eyed the vacant spot where she had left him standing moments earlier. *Though, it might not be so bad, if he did.*

-5-

Clouds of Doubt

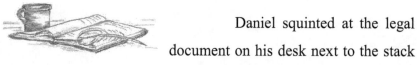 Daniel squinted at the legal document on his desk next to the stack of correspondence generated by the seasonal transactions of the farmstead. Sighing, he fell back against the finely turned spindles of his desk chair, took off his wire-rimmed spectacles and laid them next to Patrick Mooney's signature at the bottom of the proposal he had received a week earlier.

Leasing is not selling, he thought as he drew his weary eyelids down with his fingers and pulled them back toward his ears. *The land would still be Royer acres. Still yield us some benefit. But . . .*

He shook his head, pushed away from the desk and began kneading at the ache in his left hip joint with his fist. Large blue veins ridged the back of his hand as he pressed over and over this constant reminder that he was no longer a young man.

The broad wick of the oil lamp on his desk began to sputter as the last of the fuel in the reservoir burnt out in a gentle flurry of scattered light. No longer able to read the papers in the pale glow of late afternoon, Daniel grabbed the carved knobs of the chair arms and hoisted himself to his feet. He made his way to the window of his study facing south across the bulk of his land holdings, toward the horizon that held the border to Patrick Mooney's acres.

Just over the crest of the gray-green hill rising slowly to the east, the waterwheel of the family gristmill was churning out the last of the harvested grain. The stubble of fields around and beyond would lie fallow until the arduous spring planting months.

With Samuel and John gone and this traitor of a body giving up its strength, we can barely keep up, he thought.

The stomp of boots shaking away clods of dirt against the narrow stone step outside was followed by the creak of the back door in the adjacent hall. David's lanky, leathered form appeared in the study, his black hat in hand. His dark hair, stiffened by the cold air, was plastered against his forehead. The stench of the tannery, as always, confirmed his presence even before Daniel turned to see him.

"Rendering vats are starting to freeze," David announced. "Soon have to slow down operations except for the new hides from winter butchering."

"Guess we'll be losing some of your men and some field hands to the Old Forge iron works again," Daniel said.

"*Ja, Vater*," David agreed. "But many of them come back to work the farms as soon as they're able after the weather breaks. Living in that shantytown along Gap Road can be hell on earth, as I hear it. Only the charcoal burners and woodchoppers stay out there and gather huckleberries, blackberries or chestnuts to peddle in town rather than work in what they called 'civilized parts.'"

"Most of those 'swampers' came up from the South or over from Wales. Takes a rare breed for sure, to work and live in such rough conditions," said Daniel. "I'm sure Samuel makes the forge workers' lives the best he can manage up at Cove Forge with as much Christian compassion as possible, while still getting the necessary work done. The furnace is doing quite well, but not at the cost of undue suffering, I pray."

"Speaking of 'necessary work,'" echoed Jacob who appeared in the office doorway, "there's not much grain left up at the mill from this harvest." He was powdered from head to toe, his broad-brimmed hat and dark hair turned ash gray with fine flour. "More than enough labor, while it lasted. Don't know what I'd have done without Israel, especially with Thomas Fahnestock spending so much more time up in Quincy at Snow Hill Cloister instead of at the wheel. His uncle,

Andrew Fahnestock, is quite a figure among the congregants up there. Hard to miss him, with that long white beard, broad-brimmed white hat and long staff when he's out and about sharing 'the Word.'"

"Gabriel Baer said that of his 13 children, Israel's the brightest of the lot and a hard worker," said Daniel. "The Baer family's been involved with milling everything from grain to wood for as long as I can remember. "Do you think he'll want to stay on for maintenance and general labor? Won't pay as much, but then the work and hours won't be as hard, either."

"He can be high-spirited sometimes, but I think he enjoys working here well enough. It doesn't hurt that Hollinger's Wayside Tavern is just across the road for a quick stop after quitting time. I'll ask him tomorrow if he's interested," said Jacob.

"I may be able to convince some of the tannery workers, too, if you think we need them, *Vater*," offered David. "The tavern's a favorite of theirs, as well. They can get a touch of spirits there without risking their necks like they might around the blackguards who hang at Black's Corner up by the iron forge. And sometimes the Hollingers pick up news from the traveling wagons that pass through. The trick will be to keep our workers happy. Since the war ended, any young man with gumption pushes West. Extra labor is scarce and *good* laborers scarcer than hen's teeth.

"Plus, Mollie's been serving up tasty noon meals and keeping the summer house real pleasant for those who sometimes need a place to stay. They might welcome the chance to keep on working for us."

David glanced at Jacob, measuring his younger brother's reaction to his mention of Mollie.

Jacob's chest swelled slightly. "Mama and the girls are happy to lose that chore and lots of other household jobs that Mollie's taken over. With her help, they've set up for tomorrow's butcherin' in nearly half the time as other years."

"Have to admit, she's certainly proven her value to the family," added Daniel soberly. "Wasn't sure how the situation would work out after her father died. We have enough of our own family to feed and clothe as it is. Suppose it's worked out the best for everyone – so far." *Have to take care. Don't want Jacob thinking she's fit as a wife just yet. Still, at 21, it's about time he thought about marrying – and I wouldn't want Mollie to leave. Catherine and especially Elizabeth would both give me fits if that happened*, he thought.

Daniel turned his attention to the papers on his desk and Mooney's lease offer again, not anxious to spend any more time thinking about Mollie. "Have to take a serious look at how many workers we need to make the best use of the land and operations." He picked up the document and showed it to his sons. "Meantime, I'm inclined to grant Patrick Mooney a one-year lease on the 35 acres adjoining our southeast border. We'll see how that falls out after a 12-month trial and go from there." His sons nodded.

"Now, time for supper – last salt pork for awhile. After we slaughter those two gluttonous hogs tomorrow, the fresh pork and sausage'll be a welcome change."

A light frost on the corners of the windows formed oval frames around the reflections of the dining room activities as the sky darkened and the glow of hearth and candles transformed the small rectangular panes into mirrors. At Daniel's prompt from the head of the table, the other nine seated around the board bowed their heads for the blessing.

Mollie sat at the far end of the table between Nan, the youngest, and Catherine, who occupied the end seat directly opposite her husband. The power of this family moment had seized Mollie the first evening she was invited to their table. Despite minor disagreements and some tension, the family's solidarity had not lessened in the nearly three months she'd been included at their table. *Do they feel it, too?* she wondered as the prayer continued. *The strength, the confidence, so many bonded so closely together.* Daniel's deep voice evoked a memory of her father's hearty laugh. *Oh, Da, I miss you so . . . Lord, let Da know how you've blessed me. That I have a home – a family. Thank you, Lord.*

". . . in your blessed Son's name we pray," Daniel continued.

"Amen," came the unison response.

The clatter of dishes and scrape of scooping utensils took precedence until everyone had a plate in front of them brimming with fried scrapple doused in sweet, heavy corn syrup, boiled turnips and strips of smoked bacon, all crowned with a slab of fresh bread. With stomachs filled, the conversations began.

"Daniel," Catherine said, "tomorrow will be Mollie's first butchering.

Mollie blushed at the attention being shifted to her – the *adopted* child.

Daniel merely glanced at Mollie and nodded his head.

"It's pretty distressing for some folks," Jacob quietly cautioned.

"Rebecca used to hide behind the cabin when she was younger and it took me years to get over the smell," said Susan.

"But the first part's the most exciting, and the men and boys do all of that – the hauling and hanging and butchering," Cate moaned. "Then they eat a huge meal and leave to *play games* while the women and girls boil and skim the lard, grind the leavings of what isn't hung in the smokehouse and, worst of all, run their hands through yards and yards of disgusting intestines to make sure the sausages will hold when they're stuffed."

"Now Cate," Catherine said. "As I recall, no one at this table helps themselves to more sausage than you when it's offered."

"Not even Papa." Nan smiled.

Catherine looked at Mollie. "There'll be plenty of women here to get the work done. At least five families and assorted others. You can be busy all day helping without having to do so many 'disgusting' things – not on your first butchering."

"But I want to learn how, so I can really help. Like the others," Mollie protested.

"You can clean *my* buckets of innards, if you like," Susan said.

"Mine, too," said Rebecca.

"Aren't you two generous?" droned Cate.

"Now, now," said Catherine holding up her hand. "Mollie, I'll see to it that you have plenty of instruction without *intruding* on Susan and Rebecca's *fun*."

Nan tugged on Mollie's sleeve. "But the cracklin's we skim off the lard kettle are delicious."

Mollie hugged Nan. "I can hardly wait."

<h1>-6-</h1>

<h1>Sausages and Sympathies</h1>

 The Royer property was pulsing with a multitude of friends and neighbors going about the business of butchering six hogs for their year's supply of pork. Heat pouring from the split carcasses and blazing fires lessened the harsh chill of the early morning November air and saturated it with a mixture of heavy scents and discordant sounds. Large patches of the ground were darkened by the warm blood that had spurted from the slit arteries of the hogs as they hung by their back legs and dripped out their last.

After slaughtering, cleaning and cutting up the meat, the men had delivered the fluffy leaf fat and chunks of trimmings to the women. Some of the fat was pulled to use in the sausage mixture while the rest was chopped and delivered to various rendering kettles.

The organ meat and some other scraps were boiled together until they were tender enough to be moved to the puddin' kettle.

Catherine had taught Elizabeth the precise seasoning to add to the mixture that was then reduced to a thick sauce and poured into heavy earthen crocks where the hard layer of lard formed a natural seal.

As Elizabeth scooped the pieces out of the broth and into the adjacent kettle for the next step, Israel Baer swooped past with a long pointed stick and snagged the liver as it rose to the top of the roiling brew. "Best part of the hog on butchering day," he crowed as he held it steaming and dripping in the cool air. "Just needs a pinch of salt."

"Thomas Fahnestock usually claims it," said Elizabeth shooing him away playfully. "He'll be disappointed."

Catherine arrived with several sacks of cornmeal as Israel dashed away. "Can't remember the last pudding that had liver in it," she said looking at the bubbling liquid. "At least we get a rich broth for the *pon haus* before someone takes it." She dumped in the cornmeal and some salt and pepper and began stirring with a heavy wooden paddle. "This should fill at least a dozen bread tins."

"Nothing tastes better on a cold morning than a slice of fried *pon haus* covered with maple syrup," said Elizabeth. "It's one of Papa's favorites."

"Looks like that lard's ready," said Henry Reighart as he and George Smith passed by Cate who had been stirring the large steaming kettle of hot fat constantly with her mama's hefty sassafras stick.

Mollie stood near the kettle anxiously holding a large strainer ready to capture the golden brown clumps of residue floating on top. "Should be. I've been stirring for nearly half an hour. Cate says that when the cracklings turn brown, it's time to skim them off and dip the rest of the lard into the crocks. Rebecca just went to fetch an extra dipper. She says we should get some nice white lard for cooking."

George's eyes lit up at the mention of Rebecca. "Those cracklings will be tasty munching when they cool."

"So, do you know as much about butchering as you do about corn husking, Mr. Smith?" asked Rebecca as she came around the corner of the summer kitchen.

"I've helped butcher hogs every November at my home place up toward Chambersburg and just last week with two families up at Old Forge," he answered moving closer to her. "But the fat kettles at the forge were only half full. Those poor families have barely enough to eat themselves much less to fatten the one hog they might own."

Rebecca's attitude immediately softened. "What a shame." She brushed aside the rebellious dark curls that had escaped her cap with the back of her hand and glanced up at George's taller frame. "Henry told Susan that he met you when he was working on the stone buttresses with the masons at Old Forge last month. Papa says that we girls aren't to go anywhere near that place – and Mama agrees."

"Yes, things can get rough there," said George. "Henry came into the office to see Mr. Beistel, the ironmaster, when I was having a discussion with him about the company store. I was workin' up quite a lather and might have talked myself right out of my job as store manager if Henry hadn't seen what was happenin' and jumped in with some construction questions." He tipped his head toward Henry. "Couldn't help but strike up a friendship after that."

Henry strolled over to the pair. "George just needs reminded now and again that he can catch more flies with honey than vinegar. And the more flies he catches, the better things might be for the forge workers. Right, George?" Henry patted George's back.

"We'll just see how much I *catch* at the shooting competition here today," said George nudging Henry, his broad-shouldered equal, toward the far field where the other men were gathering for the matches of brawn and skill.

"I don't know about the targets on *your* side of the mountain," Henry retaliated, "but *south* of the forge, there's few that can find the mark closer than me."

"Well, don't trip for all of your struttin' on the way to the games," said Rebecca. "We'll all hear the results in a couple hours when the sweets table is spread. Now get on your way and let us women get the *real* work finished."

Ropes of pink and white speckled sausage by the yard wound around in circles inside numerous basins and buckets. The ladies got the privilege of turning the intestines inside out, scraping the mucus layer with small wooden blades and washing them clean to use as casings. Each family had their portions of pork, with some extra to be offered to the widow Hess, the traditional *metzel-sup*, for her winter larder. The second round of preparations at the Royer house was nearly complete for the late afternoon feast before the early sunset beckoned all the guests home.

The long makeshift table of split boards laid across sawhorses had been scrubbed clean of earlier business, moved to the summer kitchen, covered with a homespun cloth and was overflowing with the sweet offerings provided by all of the families who had come for the day. Pumpkin pie, apple butter cake, rhubarb pudding, cottage cheese pie and more awaited Catherine's ringing of the large cast iron bell hanging from the eave of the summer kitchen.

Mollie barely managed to make space for her pan of bread pudding between *Frau* Newcomer's Apple Brown Betty and *Frau* Geiser's Cherry Knepplies. "Hard to believe that this much food'll be gone soon," she marveled.

"It'll be like the locusts in Egypt when Mama calls them in," said Cate as she stacked some freshly rinsed tankards beside the two small kegs that would soon hold the cider simmering on the summer kitchen hearth.

Rebecca's sleeves were rolled up to her elbows as she stirred the kettle so the heavier dregs of apple wouldn't scorch and bitter the brew. Cate smiled at her as she passed by with a second armful of mugs. "That brew's flushed your cheeks *almost* as much as Henry's friend did when he was talking with you today."

"Too bad your eyes aren't as sharp as your tongue," snapped Rebecca.

"I think George Smith's handsome enough to charm almost any girl," Susan said eyeing Rebecca as she added spoons and servers to the groaning table.

"Can't say that I noticed," said Rebecca as the pace of her stirring stepped up a notch. "But I *do* admire his concern for those struggling families at the iron forge."

"Henry Reighart might not be pleased to know that *Susan* noticed George," teased Cate.

Susan jabbed a wooden paddle into the thick, rhubarb pudding. "Don't you worry about what does or doesn't please Henry," she countered. "Besides, I wonder if Israel Baer has noticed how much you enjoy *his* antics. Your eyes were practically glued to him."

Cate's mouth tightened as she glared at Susan.

Seeing she had struck a chord, Susan pressed on, "And you might soon have trouble not spillin' the milk pail or dropping the eggs. Israel just told Jacob today that since Thomas Fahnestock's up and left, he's willing to stay on working here."

"What!" Mollie nearly shouted from the door before she could stop herself.

Her reaction grabbed everyone's attention. Feeling all eyes on her, she forced a laugh and stammered, "I mean, *what* good news. Jacob can certainly use the help."

Elizabeth and Nan appeared behind Mollie with pitchers of cool milk. "Time to ring the bell, *Mutter*?" asked Nan who relished this task since she was now tall enough to reach the pull rope unassisted.

Catherine wiped her hands on her apron. "None too soon. These bickering girls are starting to try my patience." She frowned at them. "Maybe they need more work to do to spare their mouths so much flapping."

"No, Mama," the three muttered lowering their heads.

"I didn't think so," Catherine said as she smoothed some stray hairs back toward her bun. "Then, ring the bell, Nan. And watch out for the stampede."

David Royer stared at the line of lime  dust on the ground as the chorus of male voices urged the runners toward the finish. The wiry figure of Joseph Frantz whizzed past well in front of a huffing Israel Baer and the rest of the contenders. Cheers rang out for the most popular choice.

"Joseph Frantz, the winner by a mile!" announced David.

"Congratulations," said Jacob Royer, puffing as he shook Joseph's hand. "You ran a fine race, but you would've had a *real* challenge if Thomas Fahnestock hadn't moved lock, stock and barrel up to Snow Hill last week. Everyone here's been eating his dust in the races for years."

"You're right about that, Jacob," said Joseph. "You'll probably miss him at the mill, too."

"He'll be hard to replace, but Israel Baer just told me today that he'll be staying with us, a least for a while," Jacob explained.

"Did I hear my name?" asked Israel as he stooped to pick up the hat that had flown from his head during the race.

"You did," said Joseph. "Jacob just said that if Israel Baer gets to the sweets before the rest of us, we could be left licking up crumbs."

"You said that?" Israel growled at Jacob, just as the clang of the supper bell rang out across the field. Then he quickly laughed. "Well, Jacob, you're absolutely right." He dashed off toward the house with a herd of thundering boots in hot pursuit.

"Good thing the foot races come *before* the food," said Israel leaning back and spreading his hands across his stomach. "I think even a big, old snappin' turtle'd be waving his tail at me if I tried to run now."

57

Despite her sister's earlier comments, Cate's glance at Israel lingered even after the general laughter to his remark faded – long enough for her to notice that *his* glance was lingering as well, but not on her. *Who's caught his fancy?* She pondered as she followed the general direction of his stare. Suddenly the revelation struck her and her heart dropped. *Mollie! – Jacob's Mollie! Oh, no*.

Cate quickly looked away and resumed gathering empty dishes and discarded utensils from the littered table. *But Mollie's expression was odd*, she thought as she hazarded another glance at Mollie. *Sort of twisted, confused – almost like she's scared or something*.

Jacob sat across the table from Israel facing him, with Mollie to his back. The awkward exchange that Cate had witnessed was lost to him.

Just then, a splash of red-orange light streaked across the room as the door opened. "And there's the man who Joseph can thank for his win today," said Jacob pointing to Thomas Fahnestock as he closed the door behind him.

"What brings you our way this late in the day, Thomas?" asked Daniel rising from his seat to greet the late arrival.

"Not a pleasant task, I'm afraid," Thomas answered removing his black hat. "We waited as long as we could so as not to interrupt your gathering." He indicated his companion, a formidable, dark-haired figure standing just behind him. "This is David Good. His family runs the mill down on Good's Dam Road. He does milling and blacksmithing for us at Snow Hill." The young man tipped his slouched hat.

"Well, let's step into my office and you can tell me more," Daniel offered. "David and Jacob," he called searching for them in the crowd, "you should probably join us." He looked to Thomas who shook his head in agreement.

"Thank you all for your help and fellowship here today," Daniel said to the others. "Can we all bow our heads for a parting prayer before we leave you?" All tasks were paused and hands folded as he began, *"Lieber Vater im Himmel . . ."*

The light of the candle flickered on the somber faces of the five men seated around the table by the small, unlit fireplace in Daniel's study. "Now, Thomas," Daniel began, "let's hear your story and we'll see if we can help."

". . . Our best milk cow was the first to show the signs – ugly seeping sores on her mouth and hooves. We prayed it would pass, but we finally had to destroy the sickest and butchered the rest." Thomas folded his hands on the table in front of him and sighed. The lines radiating from the corners of his dark eyes and falling from the edges of his drawn mouth looked especially deep for a man in his prime. *"Herr* Royer, I know that my leaving here has caused you some trouble. I would that weren't so, but, as we discussed earlier, I must go where the Lord calls me."

The three listened respectfully and nodded.

Thomas continued, "That I'm already in your debt makes it even more difficult to ask you for more help, but what I need from you touches more folks than me. Everyone at Snow Hill's affected by the plague that's suddenly struck our dairy cows."

"It's truly a sorry sight to see," David Good offered from his place by the door in support of his friend's tale.

"God help you," said Jacob.

"Against what looks like the work of the Devil, himself." Thomas took his head in his hands and leaned forward on his elbows. "You need to know, for sure, that the contagion's contained. No other cows in the valley are at risk. But now we face the winter with no dairy cows – no milk for the butter and cheese to carry us through the season."

The formidable, but weary patriarch pushed back from the table and paced the room slowly considering his response. After a long silence, he crossed his arms over his chest and pronounced, "Tomorrow morning, I'll cut four animals from our herd. The dairy cows have been Elizabeth's first responsibility for some time now. She has a fine touch. Given the reason for the journey and the good-hearted people she'll be serving – even if they don't hear God's call exactly as we do – I feel right sending her along with you at first light to help in any way she can." He dropped his arms, looked away and cleared his throat. "We'll discuss payment in due time."

Thomas closed his eyes and tipped his head back in a silent prayer. He moved to Daniel and embraced him as a sign of gratitude and brotherhood. Daniel returned his gesture and then added, "You and your friend can spend the night and break bread with us tomorrow before leaving. God's grace be with you."

"And with you, Daniel, for your Christian love. I know the community at Snow Hill will be grateful as well," said Thomas.

"No doubt about that," added David Good. "Thomas has told me you're good people. God bless you and your family, *Herr* Royer."

-7-

Snow Hill

 Old Bessie, the most difficult personality in the group of shorthorns, had known something was up the instant Elizabeth and Susan walked through the barn door for the 4 a.m. milking. No sooner had Susan sat down beside Elsa, than Bessie tried to kick her. Only Susan's quick lunge into Elsa's soft udders kept her from getting hurt.

"These ladies know today's different," said Susan, squeezing Elsa's teats in a rhythmic splattering of warm milk into the wooden pail. "And they don't like it. No, not one little bit."

"Doesn't matter, Susan, if we like it, or they like it, or anyone else likes it. Papa's agreed to send these four from our herd with Thomas Fahnestock and his friend up to Snow Hill today. And I'm to go with them to make certain they settle in comfortably."

"When will you be back?" asked Susan trying to temper the concern in her voice. In all her 17 years, Susan couldn't recall Elizabeth spending a single night away from their farm.

"Oh, just a week. Don't worry," said Elizabeth as she patted Bessie on her broad rump and took her place at the milking stool. Soon the sound of two milkings echoed in the rafters of the chilly barn. "I need to stay 'til they've adjusted to their new home. The poor sisters and brothers at Snow Hill have been doing without milk for weeks.

"Will our cows get sick and die there, too?" asked Susan anxiously. She had grown up with Elsa, Bessie, Annalisa and Little Lulu. Even though they could be cranky, particularly if the girls were late with their twice-a-day milkings, she loved their warm breath and the way they contentedly chewed hay as they stood patiently waiting to be milked.

"Thomas told Papa they shot and buried the weakest milk cows and butchered the rest as soon as the Snow Hill sisters realized their cows were sick," Elizabeth said. "They took all the straw bedding out of the barn and burned it. They burned the pasture, too, and scattered lime all over the barnyard. Then they scrubbed every inch of the stalls with vinegar and lye soap before whitewashing the wooden stalls and stone walls. He said the barn looks almost new.

"You know, when Thomas asked Papa for the loan of some cows, I thought he might make a gift of them, especially since he's known *Herr* Fahnestock for so many years. The people at Snow Hill have always been so kind to the sick and the poor who come to the cloister for help. And *everyone* is welcome and well fed at their Love Feasts. Still, Papa gave them no special consideration. I overheard Papa tell David, 'the cows can eat the grass at Snow Hill just as well as here. Then we'll get the first calf when it's weaned, plus 20 pounds of butter.' They both had a good laugh at that," added Elizabeth with an edge of resentment.

"Papa always finds the advantage in his business dealings," said Susan. "But did he have to throw you into the bargain as well? Aren't you just a little frightened? Snow Hill has a good reputation for Christian charity, but the brothers and sisters live like monks and nuns. And they worship on Saturday, not Sunday. Don't you think that's odd?"

"Maybe, but remember what Opa Royer told us," Elizabeth reminded her. "When great-great-grandpa Sebastian came from the Rhineland, people thought he was 'odd' because he didn't believe infants knew enough about our Savior to be baptized. Some even wanted to kill him and others of our faith for that belief. We shouldn't act like them. We ought to allow these Seventh-Day German Baptists their strange ways if their *actions* are righteous."

"Suppose you're right, but will you be comfortable living with people who just work and pray all day?" Susan sighed.

Elizabeth burst out laughing. "You silly goose, what do you think *our* family does?"

"You know what I mean," said Susan in a fluster. "It's not the same. Those Snow Hill brothers and sisters are strangers living together, not kin, though the men and women properly have separate wings of the building. They might work just like us, but I hear they're *always* singing or praising God."

"We're all brothers and sisters in Christ," said Elizabeth. "The members of the cloister may find God by a different path . . . and maybe they do talk to Him a little more often than we do. Is that so wrong?"

"I guess you'll find out," said Susan.

"Yes, s'pose I will," Elizabeth answered as she lifted the heavy bucket full of milk. *Perhaps Susan is more right than she knows – perhaps.*

With Waynesburg receding in the distance, Elizabeth shivered as a trickle of icy rain dripped from the back of her bonnet and rolled down the inside of her dress.

"Are you all right back there?' Thomas Fahnestock bellowed through the furious downpour.

"*Ja, Herr Fahnestock. Alles ist gut,*" Elizabeth shouted. Retrieving the hood of her traveling cloak the strong gust had whipped from her head, she thought, *Ach, why did we have to leave in such wretched weather? Snow, rain, sleet, and fog – all since daybreak. Now thunder. What next?* She pulled her wrap tighter and

65

 repositioned herself in the saddle listening to the anguished bawling of the four Royer dairy cows. Old Bessie, the boss cow, was complaining the loudest with the others following her lead. *The Hebrew slaves taken into Egypt couldn't have raised this much ruckus,* Elizabeth thought as she pulled on Little Lulu's halter to keep her from straying off the muddy road.

Susan's earlier warning haunted her. *What if Snow Hill has wooden blocks for pillows like their founding cloister in Ephrata?* Then she relaxed some as she recalled the angelic a capella harmony she had heard years earlier at Snow Hill. *The music Papa and I heard when we passed Snow Hill could only come from godly people.*

Thomas Fahnestock led the drenched troupe through Waynesburg's Diamond, the center square, and turned at the bustling White Swan Tavern, heading north on Mechanic Street. *This street's nothing but ruts,* Elizabeth thought. *Don't know why the Schneeberger farm up ahead changed their named to Snowberger. The old Swiss name has a sweeter sound, like a beautiful snow-covered mountain,* Elizabeth imagined dreamily.

As the journey continued, her thoughts turned to the sullen stranger who had come along with Thomas to help herd the cows. He was riding some distance behind her, prodding the reluctant beasts. Elizabeth had barely caught a glimpse of David Good, the tall, dark-haired man who silently nodded when Thomas had introduced him the night before. Few words had passed during the course of the journey that would take them the better part of the day. *How's he a part of Snow Hill?* she wondered. *One of the cloister's brothers? Or maybe one of the 'outdoor members' who live nearby and worship there, but aren't celibate?*

She heard the murmur of his deep voice in conversation with Thomas. *He has strong hands*, Elizabeth recalled, *as a miller should. Maybe he grinds the fine 'Dunkard Mill' flour everyone talks about. Papa's always grumbling about the competition from Snow Hill's gristmill, how it fetches better prices than ours.* She could hear her father's very words. 'Snow Hill might be a retreat for the pious, but they don't have any objection to making a profit.'

As the three riders and the four cows gained elevation, Elizabeth felt a tug on her reins as Maggie caught the scent of stream water and hay that lay ahead. The horizon was transformed as the sun broke through the clouds and highlighted a solitary tree standing on the rise in the orderly fields. *Standing out there, doing its duty, marking the boundaries,* Elizabeth thought.

"*Ein Regenbogen*! Look a rainbow!" David Good called pointing toward the pastel colors in the sky arching above a small stone farmhouse, a bank barn and a new brick building nestled in a peaceful vale along a creek bed. "We're almost there!"

The Fabric of Life

 Elizabeth looked at the cluster of buildings sitting in a gentle hollow. She recalled the details Jacob, who had toured Snow Hill years before, had shared with her. *Just like he said,* she thought. *A farmstead much like ours. Crops in the fields, lots of sheep, a fine garden, a mill pond to feed the waterwheel, a blacksmith's forge for making nails and horseshoes and even their own cooper's shop. Everything we have and more, except the stinking tannery. And that's a blessing.*

Elizabeth was unaccustomed to spending hours in the saddle traversing muddy ground in horrid weather. The ache in her back and the twinge in her thighs lessened her concern about her new surroundings. *Believe I can face anything as long as I can get down off this horse and sit by a warm fire.*

Peter Lehman, dressed in a plain coat, pantaloons and a broad-brimmed black hat, was the first to greet the party in front of the cloister. A gaggle of gray-clad sisters wearing large bonnets and broad white handkerchiefs pinned around their shoulders followed him. He was close to her father's age, tall and solemn. *Like a Quaker, this 'Father of Snow Hill,'* Elizabeth thought.

She jumped when David Good's firm hands unexpectedly took her waist and lifted her from the saddle, setting her down amid an overwhelming swarm of eight women. She turned to thank *Herr* Good, but the handsome man had vanished with the horses as the sisters swept her through the doorway toward a blazing hearth. They took her soaking cloak and removed her wet outer traveling bonnet that was dripping onto the colorful rag rugs.

"Dear me," rose a kindly voice above the others. "You're wetter than a drowned possum. Stand by the fire while we fetch you some hot cider. Off you go, Sister Paulina! Can't you see our guest is freezing?"

Through the swirl of linen skirts, the smell of damp wool and the clucking of the sisters, Elizabeth caught sight of the diminutive sister who issued the orders. Bent nearly in half, the older woman walked stiffly, joining Elizabeth at the hearth. *Must be rheumatism, poor thing,* thought Elizabeth. The pain of each step was etched in the woman's face, but sunshine filled her voice.

"Welcome to Snow Hill, *Fräulein* Royer. I'm Sister Melonia."

Later that night, Sister Melonia led Elizabeth to a room of her own in the women's wing. A flickering candle revealed a comfortable rope bed with a tick mattress, plenty of covers and, to her relief, a fluffy down pillow. As Melonia set the beeswax candle on the bedside stand, she noticed Elizabeth's expression.

"No, you won't find any wooden block pillows here," Melonia said.

How did she know? Elizabeth thought.

"We owe much to our mother cloister in Ephrata. But to my mind," Melonia explained kindly, "they live the life the Lord has so graciously given them too severely. Our brothers and sisters to the East prefer the 'lean and hungry look,' but you'll find nothing but ample cheese, honey, ham and all nature's delights on our table. We see little virtue in worshipping God while shivering in the dark with half-empty bellies."

Elizabeth smiled. Melonia smoothed the coverlet, straightening its bright geometric patterns. "The great bell in the cloister's belfry rings 20 minutes before five, and the Royer cows, accustomed as they may be to an earlier milking time, will have to wait until we've had morning prayers and a hearty breakfast in the *Saal. Gute Nacht*, my dear." Melonia closed the door lightly behind her.

Exhausted, Elizabeth blew out the candle, pulled the woven coverlets to her chin, and despite the creaking of the bed, fell immediately to sleep. The next sound she heard was the insistent clanging that signaled a new day.

The first two days passed in a blur. Elizabeth was shy in the beginning, careful to discern the house rules, taking everything in and hoping to avoid doing anything that might disrupt in the sisters' finely

70

tuned routine. They had treated her like a distinguished visitor and welcomed her to the upstairs *Saal,* a large open room filled with long oak benches where members of the order worshipped together – men always on the right side, women on the left. Elizabeth occasionally wondered how her family was managing without her, but the cloister's daily rhythm of work and prayer was soothing. *Susan'll never believe me, but I feel really comfortable here,* she thought.

"The cows suffered terribly," said Melonia as she walked with Elizabeth to the barn in the dawn's light. "In the beginning we were puzzled. They were feverish, giving less milk. Because I'm closer to the ground than the others, I was the first to notice the small yellow blisters in their mouths and the pus coming from the ulcers on their feet. Pitiful." Melonia shook her head. "They tried to eat the Timothy grass, but their mouths were too tender and by that time they had little appetite. The blisters near their hooves caused them so much pain they laid down in the pasture and couldn't get up, even to come back to the barn. When long strings of drool began to stream from their mouths, we knew they had the wasting hoof-and-mouth disease."

"Was there no hope?" asked Elizabeth, holding the barn door open for Melonia.

"No, dear." Melonia looked tenderly toward the 'new' cows. "We made poultices of moist clay and washed their hooves with an astringent made from white oak bark. I applied a salve made with herbs from the garden, mostly to ease their discomfort, but with no chance of recovery, Brother Fahnestock had to shoot them.

The new arrivals mooed at their visitors.

"Daisy was my favorite," Melonia said. "She gave the sweetest milk, and silly as this may sound, she was like a child to me. I can still hear the echo of the rifle shot." She bowed her head as Elizabeth waited silently.

"Well, enough of this." Melonia said using the edge of her apron to brush away a tear. "Introduce me to your precious ones. Who likes to have their ears scratched and which one do we need to keep our eye on?"

"This one in particular doesn't like sudden movements," said Elizabeth gently patting Bessie's broad head."

"Ah, yes. Slow as they are to move when you're in a hurry, they can kick quick as lightning. I've worn many a bruise from a well-placed hoof," said Melonia. "Soon we'll be able to take measure of their mood by the swish of a tail or the twitch of an ear."

"And as you surely know," added Elizabeth, "it always helps to be calm. If you're upset for any reason, they'll sense it."

"How true," Melonia nodded. "As my father used to say, 'Happy farmer, happy cows.'"

-8-

Elizabeth's New Visions

Elizabeth quickly became accustomed to the cloister's daily routine. *Not so different than my life at home,* thought Elizabeth as she fetched what remained of the dwindling supply of butter from the cool cellar. The structure had been built right over a spring and the sisters stored rounds of cheese on sturdy shelves and set crocks of their precious butter on stone slabs in troughs brimming with icy spring water. *Pastor Lehman assigns specific tasks every morning just like Papa. The brothers work hard all morning in the field or at the mill just like David and Jacob and the sisters scrub floors, work in the garden and cook just like Mama and the girls.*

After dinner and a brief worship service with more singing, the brothers retired to their private rooms and the sisters settled into their wing of the cloister. *They work just as hard as we do,* Elizabeth considered, *but somehow they have more free time.*

The Fabric of Life

The hours between evening prayer and bedtime belonged to the individuals themselves. Elizabeth was surprised and impressed. *Mama always makes sure we don't waste a moment. Even reading the Bible's a privilege. Everyone here works for each other and shares everything — without any payment.*

In the evening, some of the women gathered in the sitting room around a wood fire blazing inside the 10-plate stove. Sister Hannah spent her time quietly stitching small pieces of dyed cotton together to construct a beautiful quilt. Sister Zenobia, the most artistic  of all, created exquisite *frakturs* and illuminated manuscripts with pen and colored inks by the light of a whale oil lamp. *So skillful,* Elizabeth thought. *Each letter's made with a single stroke of the pen.*

"Would you like to try?" asked Sister Zenobia offering her the pen. "I'm copying some of Brother Obed's poetry."

"Oh, no thank you, Sister," said Elizabeth. "I'm better with the spindle." She busied herself spinning wool to repay, in part, the community's hospitality. She watched Melonia, leaning forward in her rocking chair, poring over musical scores. Multiple clefs in the margins and unusual dots covered the sheets of paper. Elizabeth peeked at the musical notes and thought, *They sing the five- and sometimes seven-part harmony so effortlessly. The women, especially the strong sopranos, lead the melody.* Elizabeth smiled to herself.

74

Men don't give up control very often in church affairs. Maybe that's why the music sounds so sweet to me.

Melonia, absorbed in her study of *die Notenbücher,* moved her tightly pursed lips softly rehearsing her part. Elizabeth admired her new friend's concentration. *Ja,* she thought, pulling the rough woolen fiber with her fingers. *Melonia ist meine Freundin. In such a short time, feels as if I've known her forever – like Polly and Mollie.* She sighed and studied Melonia's tranquil face. *Her pain makes her look so much older than 40 years, but she never complains. Even tries to hide the blindness in her one eye.*

Melonia, aware of Elizabeth's curious gaze, looked up and smiled. "I'm reading from our hymnal, *The Song of the Turtle-Dove.* The full title's *The Song of the Lonely and Abandoned Turtle-Dove,* but I prefer the shorter version because not all our songs are mournful." She winced. "Oh, my. Time to move these stiff joints of mine. Follow me, I want to show you something."

Elizabeth set aside the spindle. *What could it be?* She followed Melonia up the corner staircase to the attic of the brick building and through a storeroom filled with several *Kists* arranged in neat rows.

Melonia sat down on the edge of one of the walnut dower chests to catch her breath. "This one's mine," she said setting down the punched tin lantern and stroking the smooth wood lovingly. "My father made this for me thinking I'd one day be a bride. Little did he know I'd choose to become a bride of Christ. Even so, this *Kist* and all my personal belongings came with me when I joined the Order. I was only 17. All of these things belong to the cloister now, to all of us. But what I brought is mine to take back if I ever decide to leave. Imagine that," she said. "Why would I ever go away when I'm so happy here?"

"But the chest reads 'Lydia?'" Elizabeth said admiring the painted yellow birds and scrolled blue cornflowers encircling the name.

"Lydia was the birth name my parents gave me. When I joined Snow Hill, I chose Melonia. Do you think it suits me?"

"Melonia." Elizabeth said softly rolling the syllables on her tongue. "Reminds me of 'melody.' It suits your love of music very well."

"You *are* a sweet child of God, Elizabeth. I *do* have the heart of a musician. But," Melonia wrapped her gnarled fingers around Elizabeth's hand and looked at her palm, "I see that *you* have the hands of a healer." She then traced the long lifeline on Elizabeth's right hand. "You have many years ahead of you. How will you use them?"

"What do you mean?" asked Elizabeth puzzled by a concept she had never considered before.

"How will you choose to live the rest of your life?" Melonia explained.

Elizabeth's thoughts flew in circles. *Choose? I have a choice?*

76

"Well," Elizabeth faltered retrieving her hand trying to hide the sudden shaking. "My place is taking care of my parents and brothers and sisters." An image of her older brother's scowl flashed in her mind. *David's so nasty, he'll never find a woman to marry. He'll expect me to look after him.* "I've not been inclined toward marriage," she continued sheepishly. "I mean, I'm nearly 30, too old to . . ."

"To what?" said Melonia, raising an eyebrow.

Elizabeth said nothing.

Melonia sensed Elizabeth's hesitation and embarrassment. "I understand, child, but remember, God sometimes chooses paths for us we may not have planned. Don't worry if you don't have an answer now. In His time, God will show you the way." Melonia rose and pushed open a door to another room. She led Elizabeth into a small empty space with high dormer windows.

"This is where I come when I have troubling questions for the Master. We call it the prayer room. I come here to meditate and discern God's will more clearly." Her breath hovered in the frosty air. "Away from the others, away from the world."

Elizabeth tightened her shawl against the chill of the attic. Then Melonia with surprising ease pulled on some heavy ropes with dangling iron cylinders attached at the opposite end and a section of the roof between the stout rafters above them creaked open revealing a magical slice of night sky sprinkled with a multitude of twinkling stars. Elizabeth raised her head in wonder and twirled slowly, mystified by the sparkling grandeur overhead.

"One of our most clever brothers contrived these balanced weights to lift a section of the roof so we could worship God under the stars. With the firmament above and the earth beneath, it's the perfect place to come when the life of the spirit and the call of the world confounds me. "The bend in my spine keeps me from gazing skyward, but the memory of those stars is as vivid now as when I first saw them. God be praised."

Elizabeth was lost in her own reverie beyond Melonia's words.

"Well, then, I'll leave you to your conversation with the Lord," she whispered. She placed the small glowing lantern on the floor and departed.

How long have I been here? Elizabeth wondered looking up into the night. She then glanced at the flickering lantern and continued to ponder her future. *Could I join the sisters here, a life of praise and contemplation? Precious little to bring with me, for sure, But so many hours to call my own. How better to devote myself to God?*

She imagined her father's uncomprehending face and her mother's pained expression if she were to tell them she was leaving. *'What!' Papa'd shout. 'No daughter of mine will abandon the faith of our fathers to become a Sabbatarian. You'll not abandon our family and throw your life away.'*

"It's hopeless," she murmured. "Lord, why did you bring me here to tempt me with a life I can't claim?" She gazed anew at the open roof and the stars sparkling through her tears. With a sigh, she gathered up her skirt, cast one last look about the empty room, retrieved the sputtering lantern and made her way downstairs to bed.

David Good removed his hat, placed it on a wall peg and brushed his dark hair back from his forehead revealing his full cheeks and chestnut eyes. He took his place among the brothers at the community's Sabbath service. Individuals and families who lived nearby often joined the cloister's residents in worship.

Elizabeth felt his eyes on her as he settled onto the long oak bench on the opposite side of the *Saal*. Without thinking, she smiled at him. When he smiled back, a pleasant warmth filled her. *Such a large congregation, the 'outsiders' and 'Solitaries,' and so many children with their parents,* she thought as she looked around the large room. *Feels strange to worship on Saturday. Mama and the girls are baking bread and preparing food right now, and Papa and the men are hurrying to get as much done as they can before Sunday Meeting. Work's finished here by sundown Friday. The rest of the world's going about its Saturday business, while we're here honoring the Sabbath just as the Hebrews did.*

Pastor Lehman began reading the scripture. Elizabeth recognized the familiar passages from Isaiah thinking, *Why should something as unimportant as whether Saturday or Sunday was the Lord's Day divide us?* She observed the reverent faces around her. *Some people even accuse these devout folk of breaking the law because they labor on Sunday. Maybe it's 'odd,' but should they be punished for being different?*

After the service, the clear blue sky drew Elizabeth toward the hill beyond the barn. She passed by the sisters as they chattered happily and served the crowd healthy portions of pork and sauerkraut along with Snow Hill's famed cucumber pickles. An impressive crowd stood outside the building waiting for the community meal.

Catching sight of a scruffy looking man who was first in line for an ample helping, Elizabeth pulled Melonia aside. "I know him," she whispered. "He's a tramp Papa turned away last month when he came 'round begging for food. Papa said he's poor because he's lazy and won't work for his daily bread. Shouldn't Snow Hill be more careful about who they help?"

Melonia smiled. "Everyone's welcome at our table. We share what we have with all. People expect such generosity from us. Some folks even think we're a Catholic convent and call Snow Hill 'the Nunnery.' No matter, all are welcome here."

Elizabeth knew Melonia hadn't meant to criticize her papa, but the charity she had described was distinctly different from his Christianity. *Papa believes 'God helps those who help themselves,'* Elizabeth pondered. *But the sisters and brothers help everyone without question.* She felt uneasy. *I need to be alone,* she thought as she moved away and up the hill following a red-tailed hawk skimming the treetops to alight in the spindly branches of the witness tree she had seen from afar the first day she arrived.

"Confusing isn't it?" said a deep voice.

Elizabeth turned quickly to discover that David Good had wandered up the slope behind her.

"What?' Elizabeth said, hiding both her surprise and pleasure at seeing him again.

"These *Siebentagers* – Seven Dayers – and all this business of worshipping on Saturday. Since God is Lord of Time, you'd think Saturday or Sunday would make no difference."

Elizabeth caught the glint of humor in his eyes and returned the look. "*Das stimmt, Herr* Good. You make an excellent point."

"Still the Snow Hill kindred are kind souls." He stepped closer, encouraged by her smile. "Their singing's wonderful, isn't it?

Truth is that's one reason I attend services here. One day I heard their voices when was traveling to Mont Alto and I was so moved by the sound that for weeks I'd hide at the edge of the woods just to listen. When I learned they needed a blacksmith, I offered my services. I've been worshipping here ever since."

"Have you thought about joining the Brotherhood?" asked Elizabeth hesitantly.

"Oh," David fumbled. "Oh, no . . . I could never be one of the Solitaries . . . I mean. Their way's not my calling."

"I didn't know much about their different ways 'til I came, but I have to admit, theirs is a gentle way of life," said Elizabeth. "Kind of like a large family, but . . ." She tilted her head searching for the right words.

". . . without the discord," said David finishing her sentence.

They looked at one another, paused and then burst out laughing.

"I know a lot about big families. There are nine of us," said David. "You don't remember me, but I'm one of the Goods from the mill on Good's Dam Road just south of your farm. I saw you once when my papa sent me looking for an extra grindstone to replace one at our gristmill. Your brother Jacob was very helpful."

"Glad you dealt with Jacob instead of Papa," said Elizabeth, immediately putting a hand to her mouth. "Oh, I shouldn't have said that. My time away has made me careless with my words."

David looked down at his well-worn boots. "No need to apologize for your father doing business wisely. We all have to make a living," he said. "No harm in that. Particularly since running farms and mills has gotten harder. *Herr* Royer's a well-respected steward of the bounty God's given him.

Times are tough. I'm one of the younger sons in my family. I realized long ago I have to look out for myself. Space around our big table's getting tighter and the mill will go to my older brother one day. Third sons like me have to make their own opportunities."

"Is that why you're here?" asked Elizabeth.

"Partly. The cloister's mill's doing very well, but the brothers are getting older. I grind grain, shoe the horses, forge nails, and in winter, help make barrels in the cooper's shop. Life here runs at a quieter pace, but there's no less work."

"It's pleasant here," said Elizabeth smiling.

David cleared his throat. "Then you may not like what I've come to tell you. *Herr* Fahnestock told me he wants to escort you back to Waynesburg on our way to market in Baltimore." He allowed the news to sink in. "We leave in the morning."

Elizabeth's smile faded. "I'll be happy to see my mother and sisters again, but truly, I'll miss the people here, Melonia especially." She gently folded her hands together.

David moved a step closer and looked directly into her eyes. "*Fräulein* Elizabeth, I hope Melonia's not the only one you'll miss."

-9-

Matters of the Heart

Elizabeth had barely disappeared up the lane with her bundle of essentials, Thomas Fahnestock and the four cows bound for Snow Hill, than Daniel announced that he would leave for Cove Forge the following day. Two fewer persons in the Royer household meant less food to prepare, but the weight of daily work remained, minus two able pairs of hands to help. Some of the seasonal hires had remained, but even with the additional manpower, the somewhat more idle time of winter was still weeks away.

Production, though slowed, still kept David busy at the tannery. In addition to mending fences and repairing buildings, Jacob and Israel journeyed daily to either the large woodlot some five miles away to help with the sawmill activities or to cut and haul heavy limestone rocks to the farmstead's kiln for firing. And there could never be too much split wood for the manor house and summer kitchen's nine fireplaces.

"At least this cold spell has hardened the dirt and mud. Makes pulling these carts much easier," said Cate whose mittened hands were behind her back and hooked around the handle next to Mollie's grip on the 4 x 4-foot wooden cart as they shared the load. Four ponderous grain bags packed with the fine, white lime they had just gathered at the family kiln were slumped in the cart bed. Nearly a mile separated the kiln from the barn where the bags were stored.

"Leave it to Cate to find the one sweet cherry among the sours," said Susan who struggled likewise with Rebecca at her side dragging a second cart. "And she and Mollie even have one more bag in their cart than we do."

"Leaves room for the last of the cabbage and squash," Rebecca reminded her. "Remember, Mama told us to make one last sweep of the four-square garden before the frost goes too deep."

"Still more sauerkraut?" asked Mollie.

"You'll be surprised how fast those big crocks get emptied this winter," Cate explained. "Lots more cold days here than where you came from, Mollie."

"It feels as if that was a lifetime ago," Mollie sighed. "So much has happened."

"We emptied the kiln just in time," said Susan. "Look who's coming up the hill." About two hundred yards ahead of them, Jacob was astride the family mule, Siggy, pulling a drag sled loaded with large chunks of quarried limestone. Riding on top was Israel Baer.

"Keep your eyes in your head, Cate," Rebecca teased, calling attention once again to her younger sister's supposed infatuation with the dashing Israel.

"You're like a dog with a favorite bone," Cate countered. "Just can't let go, even if there isn't any meat to it."

As the mule got closer, Cate caught Susan's eye as they both watched carefully for Mollie's reaction to the two handsome young men. Cate had shared with Susan the exchange she had witnessed between Israel and Mollie at the butchering supper. They had then recalled the long black hair they had seen months earlier when Mollie had dashed away from the graveyard with her *friend* – the same dark hair, perhaps, that now rested on the shoulders of Jacob's passenger. The girls had agreed not to mention their suspicions to anyone else, especially Rebecca.

"Glad to see you beat us to the kiln," said Jacob as he pulled Siggy to a stop beside the two carts. "Now Israel and I can put this load right in for the next firing. We need lots of extra lime to whitewash Samuel's old cabin for the new tenants in the spring. You didn't roll off back there, did you, Brother?" he hollered over his shoulder.

Propped against the largest rock with his back to the girls, Israel pulled up speechless when he turned to answer Jacob and discovered they had company. "I . . . I . . . uh," he stammered as Mollie faltered ever so slightly and then occupied herself by making unnecessary adjustments to the bags of lime in the cart.

"The ride must've shaken the words right out of him," Jacob laughed as he hopped to the ground to help Mollie. "It's rare when Israel doesn't have something to say."

Israel shrugged and turned his back again – so unlike his usual gregarious nature. Jacob didn't notice as he concentrated on inspecting the four heavy bags with Mollie. "They look pretty secure to me, Mollie," he advised. "But they're really heavy. Do you want Israel and me to help you unload them?"

"Oh, no," she answered abruptly as Israel squirmed a bit where he sat. Jacob tilted his head, momentarily perplexed.

Sensing the undercurrent of discomfort, Cate piped up. "We heaved them all *into* the carts without any trouble. Getting them *out* at the barn won't be nearly as hard." Mollie's expression relaxed, grateful for Cate's intrusion.

"Cate's right," added Susan. "You two fellas have enough to do already. No need for you to backtrack and waste your time when the days are so short as it is."

"Have to agree, I suppose. Sun's setting in a hurry lately," Jacob relented giving Mollie one last look. "Are you sure?"

Mollie nodded and smiled slightly.

Jacob lifted himself back aboard the mule and clicked his tongue. As the drag sled passed by the carts, Susan witnessed a brief, but painful glance pass between Mollie and Israel – the same wistful, bittersweet look Cate had described to her earlier.

The last bag of lime thunked against the pile already provisioned in the barn. Pale puffs floated in the chill air as the girls panted. Susan adjusted her heavy woolen cape and grabbed Mollie's arm. "Time for your last gardening lesson 'til spring." Then she eyed her sister and partner in shared intrigue. "Cate, you and Rebecca can go back and help Mama. Mollie and I'll store the carts and gather the last vegetables from the four-square garden."

"*Gut*," said Cate. "It's getting colder by the minute."

A sizeable harvest of golden, silky-skinned onions, lightly marbled green heads of cabbage and a few bulbous purple-topped turnips soon lay beside the gate to the four-square garden. Drying stalks and crinkled, curling leaves now spread throughout the once tidy 66 x 66-foot sectioned garden. Having given up the last of the season's harvest, all that remained was the final gathering of the forage to add to the growing compost heap.

"Last bed to check is the acorn squash," Susan instructed. "It's easy to miss them. After the leaves turn yellow, they blend right in."

Mollie headed in the direction Susan indicated. Kneeling at the far corner of the section, she clawed back a clump of debris with one hand and plucked a large pear-shaped squash with the other. "Look! I found one!"

As Mollie added it to the others, Susan seized on the opportunity she had been waiting for. "*Jacob* will be pleased. Buttered acorn squash is one of his favorites. And knowing that *you* picked it will make it even tastier for him." She spoke the line very deliberately and stared at Mollie.

Mollie's shoulders fell as she faced Susan. *Does she know?* Mollie's mind raced. *How? . . . What do I say? . . . What do I really feel?* Tears began to well in her eyes. *I can't . . . I can't say it.* She moved past Susan and slumped to the ground with her back against the fence and covered her face with her hands.

Susan sat down beside her and waited. After a pause she whispered, "It's all right, Mollie. Whatever it is, it'll be all right."

"But it's not," Mollie murmured. "Jacob is such a fine man. You and your family have been so kind to me." She picked up the squash and turned it over in her hands. "I'm just a swamper – not good enough for him anyway. Not for a Royer – the son of such a respected family."

Susan frowned and shook her head. "Don't talk like that, Mollie. You . . ."

"Even if *Herr* Royer *did* accept me – if Jacob wanted me. Oh, Susan . . ." Teardrops slid down the smooth rind of the squash. "He deserves someone who loves him and no other. Someone as fine as he is." Her voiced cracked.

Susan hugged her. "Maybe we can't help who we love. Sometimes we can't understand how the Lord works. We . . ."

"Israel and I have tried," she sobbed. "He knows that I *need* to love Jacob – to do what Da would have wanted. Since Da died, we've tried to . . . to stay apart . . . to . . ."

The squash rolled away as Mollie returned Susan's hug and wept on her shoulder.

Nan grinned as she rolled up the sleeves of her dress. On the floured board in front of her, two large pottery bowls swelled high above their rims with warm, yeasty bread dough. Catherine stood next to her soaking in her youngest daughter's childhood glee. *Every one of my girls loved this part of the baking,* she thought.

Nan determined her target, drew her elbow up above her ear and plunged her fist into the center of the mound closest to her. It instantly deflated. Nan brushed her hands together in triumph and pulled the second bowl toward her as Catherine dumped the contents of the first onto the powdered surface and began the second kneading.

The kitchen door suddenly flew open behind them as Rebecca dove in headlong catching herself on the edge of the table between them.

"Whoa, *Tochter*. Where's the fire?" asked Catherine.

Rebecca's smile stretched from ear to ear. "You might want to make a few extra loaves – and maybe an apple pie – and some pretzels – and . . ."

"What are you talking about, Rebecca?" said Nan. "We . . ."

"I'm talking about Papa!" Rebecca interrupted. "He's coming down the lane. But, best of all, *Samuel's* with him – and some of his little ones."

Without a pause, Catherine took a step back and began looking around the small winter, work kitchen compiling a list of necessities in her head to accommodate the sudden influx of family. Then she allowed herself a moment of euphoria as she crossed her arms over her chest and spun in a circle. "What a wonderful surprise!" Then she hugged both girls to her. "We're so blessed." She considered the glistening dough piles wilting onto the board. "Now, Rebecca, take over for me. I'll fetch Mollie from the summer kitchen. Not a minute to lose if we're to give a fit welcome."

That evening the family gathered in the parlor soaking in one another's company.

"I just got 'tensies,' Papa. I won!" squealed young Daniel, cross-legged on the floor in the flickering halo of the hearth.

"*Gute Arbeit, mein Sohn*," Samuel responded as he stood looking out the front window at the familiar scene from his youth now dimmed both by the early sunset and the passing of six winters since he had moved away.

"You're an excellent jack-stones player for a 7-year-old," Nan said smiling as she gathered the small, pronged playing pieces and wooden ball together for the next round. "And I imagine you've managed a fine collection of clay marbles as well from shooting matches with your friends in Cove Forge."

Well," young Daniel boasted, "Papa *did* allow me to bring my leather pouch along for our visit. I'll show them to you tomorrow."

"And Jane will soon have a fine pot holder to give her mama," added Catherine, seated at the small game table with her granddaughter whose long pigtails fell nearly to her waist as they dangled from under her small white cap. "She's really taken to this little hand loom that all of her aunts once used."

"And I'm only five." The child smiled up at Catherine. "Maybe I can teach Henrietta how to weave when she gets older." The corners of her mouth dropped. "I wish she didn't wear nappies

92

anymore. Then she might have been able to come with Daniel and Papa and me."

"I'm sure she'll make it next time, along with Mama and your new brother Benjamin. When everyone is bigger and stronger, like you and young Daniel are now," Samuel reassured her.

But not our John, thought Catherine. *I doubt he'll ever choose to spend time at home with his father. Not after that awful war drove them apart – the terrible things they said.*

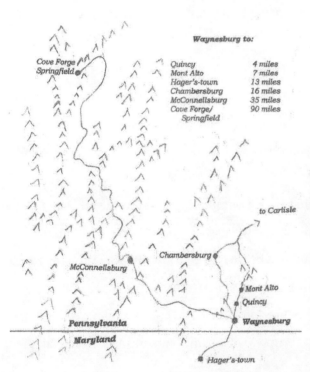

Waynesburg to:

Quincy	4 miles
Mont Alto	7 miles
Hager's-town	13 miles
Chambersburg	16 miles
McConnellsburg	35 miles
Cove Forge/ Springfield	90 miles

"It's a long journey from Cove Forge," said Susan as she laid her needlework hoop on her lap. Rebecca and Cate sat next to her on the settee, each busily sewing items to be put away in their *kists* for their future homes after they married.

"It took three days this trip with the wagon along," the elder Daniel announced from his place in the large upholstered wing chair to the right of the fireplace. He closed his eyes and rolled his head. "Every year older makes the trip ten miles longer."

David made his way into the parlor and took a seat at the mahogany secretary with its numerous drawers. "Accounts from the forge are very encouraging, Samuel. I only have a few questions about . . ."

"More about that tomorrow," said Daniel adjusting his posture and surveying the room. "In fact, I believe devotions are in order so we can all find a place to lay our heads for the night. Susan, go find Mollie so that we can commence. Now that she shares our roof, she should share our prayers as well – as best she can."

"Yes, Papa." Susan tucked her embroidery into the basket on the floor beside the rocking chair. "She keeps working until we stop her most days," she explained to Samuel as she went in search of Mollie.

"Don't know what I'd do without her," Catherine added.

"Sounds like this young woman is quite an asset," Samuel said directing his gaze at Jacob who sat on the low platform rocker near the fire watching the third round of jack-stones.

Jacob returned his brother's look. "I think we all agree on that. She . . ." He stopped abruptly as Mollie and Susan arrived at the arched doorway.

"Sorry I'm late," Mollie explained as she knelt to the floor alongside Susan's rocker. Eyes lowered, she concentrated her attention on arranging her skirt, trying to be as unobtrusive as possible.

"I'm glad we have your help to keep up with the housework," said Nan. "Now that December's come, we never know when Belsnickel might rattle the doors with his bag of treats and sticks." She smiled in Jane's direction whose eyes widened at the  thought of the mischievous elf. "A slice of his sweet honey cake or sugared nuts – Yum! What do you think, Jane?" she asked.

"I think I'd like to help you with your chores tomorrow," Jane answered anxiously. "I've heard that he has an awful helper, Pelznickel who gives the sticks to parents if their children have been lazy."

"Enough," said Daniel opening the family Bible on his lap. "The gifts of our Lord are better remembered now." The room fell silent as hands folded below bowed heads. "Let us welcome Samuel and his children home with this reading from Genesis. . . . *And behold I am with thee, and will keep thee whither thou goest, and will bring thee again to his land . . .*"

-10-

Tough Choices – Hard Answers

"So *meine Liebchen*, you had a fine time, did you?" asked Samuel seated on the bench of the family's small wagon. He turned and tipped his hat as he pulled away from his in-laws' house in Waynesburg. Young Daniel and Jane, wrapped in woolen blankets in the wagon bed, waved goodbye furiously to their *Oma* and *Opa* Provines who stood on the front porch.

"Oh yes, Papa!" Jane hugged a floppy rag doll with a tangle of yarn hair and bone button eyes, one with a chipped edge, to her chest. "*Oma* said that Mama carried this doll with her everywhere when she was my age."

Daniel tugged on the leather strap dangling from the arms of a large wooden "Y" he gripped in his hand. "And we can have some fine target matches with this great slingshot *Opa* Provines and I carved in his cooper shop."

"*Sehr gut*, said Samuel. "Now bundle up and busy yourselves with your new toys. We'll talk more later. Right now *Tante* Susan and

I are going to visit a bit." He switched both reins to his left hand and gave Susan, who was seated beside him, a quick squeeze with his right arm. "I'm glad Mama had some errands for you in town, *Schwester*. This gives us some time to catch up. Now, tell me about this Henry Reighart."

Susan's face warmed in spite of the chill air. "I've not really said this to anyone else," she said in hushed tones glancing back to ensure that the children weren't listening, "but Henry is *wunderbar*." Samuel smiled at her as she continued. "He's a fine stonemason – works very hard – and never complains. He's strong and handsome and sweet and . . . and . . . he makes me laugh." She bowed her head slightly. "And, best of all, his face lights up when he sees me. He cares for me as much as I do him, I believe."

"I thought as much," Samuel said, "but hearing you speak leaves no doubt in my mind. I'm so happy for you, Susan. I'll never forget how you and Rebecca helped Sarah and me when we hit some rough spots early on. And speaking of Rebecca, I hear that she's been smiling more than usual lately when a certain George Smith is around."

"Too early to really tell about that," said Susan. "But Henry says George is a respectable man and I trust his judgment. Rebecca's not ready to talk about it yet. We'll just have to wait and see. He's the company office clerk at Old Forge, so he's familiar with the hard life at an iron works, just like you. He was a teamster until one of those Kentucky mules did a permanent injury to his leg."

"And difficult iron working is, for sure," Samuel agreed. "But tell me about Elizabeth now. She may have returned from Snow Hill by the time we get home. Has anyone caught her eye or is she still more focused on Heaven?"

"She's mourned Polly's passing more than any of us, but I'm hoping *this* world's been looking brighter to her. Mollie Null's been the best medicine for Elizabeth," Susan explained. "She's got Polly's energy and good humor."

"And Jacob's heart?" Samuel asked.

"That, too," Susan admitted hesitantly.

"Do I sense a problem?" Samuel flicked the reins to urge Maggie up the final hill before the descent to the entrance to their lane. The late afternoon sun cast a long shadow on the dirt road in front of them.

"All I can say is pray for them both, Samuel. I fear they may not be as fortunate as Henry and me. Only God knows what will be, but . . ." She shook her head. "I can say no more."

"That's a snow sky if ever I saw one," remarked Daniel to his sons as he glanced out the window of his study.

"And I noticed the hogs pushing up sizeable nests of hay – sure sign we're due for more than just a dusting," added David. "Hope the hired help  make it in tomorrow before the storm hits. We could use the extra hands dragging paths to the outbuildings and woodlot. Once they're here, they can stay on in the summer kitchen until it's safe to travel."

"I've already convinced Israel to stay the night in the summer kitchen, so we can count on him for tomorrow," said Jacob staring into the small fire flickering in the hearth. "With so many siblings at his house, I think he probably enjoys the quiet here."

"I nearly forgot how much work it is to keep this place going," said Samuel. "Forging iron is backbreaking, never-ending work – hauling all of those trees and charcoal and pig iron – keeping the furnaces fired night and day, every day, but all of *these* acres are just as demanding."

"It's harder for the family to keep up anymore." Daniel crossed his arms over his chest. "With two fewer sons at home and far less strength of my own, we've had to depend more and more on outsiders, paid laborers and indentured servants. We've leased substantial acres to neighbors for a percentage of the crops and, Samuel, your old cabin will definitely have a tenant by next spring."

"Such letting go must gnaw at you, *Vater*," said Samuel. "The complicated choices I'm forced to make all too often at the forge mat up my mind like burdock burrs in a sheep's neck." He began to pace the room. "If the furnace doesn't make a quality

product and a profit, we'll have to shut down. What would the workers do then? But to maintain the operation, I have to push the men so hard for so little. The best I can do is to make certain everyone has shelter and no one goes hungry. We started a small school for the younger children, and a doctor stops by once a month, but . . ."

"The shantytown that's built up along Gap Road up at Old Forge for the workers and their families is a sorry sight. I suspect that *Herr* Bietsel, the ironmaster, may not be as conscientious or considerate as you," said Daniel.

Elizabeth peeked her head around the corner from the hall. "Mama says that the food's ready when you are, Papa." She beamed at Samuel. "There's barely elbow room at the table. What a pleasant problem!"

"Tell Mama we're on our way." Daniel swept the air with his hands herding Jacob and Samuel toward the door.

The business of eating was clearly over and table conversations had wound down, but none of the 12 Royers, from 54-year-old Daniel to 5-year-old granddaughter Jane, made a move to leave. As they settled back into their chairs, a palpable sense of unity, a special bond of family passed from member to member. Knowing glances around the table affirmed a subtle but deeply felt understanding. The sharing knew no age or gender.

Mollie was the only exception, though not deliberately so. She held her shoulders tensely and pushed the last bite of flaky pie crust around on her plate observing the moment. *They've given me so much. I've done my best to earn my place here – to belong – to be Elizabeth's sister – to love Jacob – to . . .* She forced the final morsel into her mouth and chewed slowly to help quiet the tears that threatened to betray her sense of isolation, but as she swallowed, the sadness overwhelmed her.

She dropped her hands to her lap and felt the three shillings – her weekly wages – in her apron pocket. Daniel had given them to her before the meal. *No one else is paid for their work,* she thought. *It's kind of Herr Royer, but . . . it reminds me that I'm hired help, not family. I'd rather work for nothing.*

She pushed back slowly from the table. *Can't let them see me cry. Can't ruin this time for them.* "Summer kitchen hearth needs tending," she whispered. As she had hoped, all the Royers remained intent on each other. She pivoted slowly, rose from her chair and slipped out of the room – *their* room – to find her place in the world.

Israel sat in front of the summer kitchen fireplace wrapped in a coarse blanket from the sleeping pallet rubbing his calloused hands together and thinking. His dark hair hung in a ponytail at the base of his neck. *She's in there with them now – and I'm out here.* He picked up a stray chip of bark and tossed it at the spitting flames. *Staying here changes nothing.* His shoulders drooped forward as he studied the flickering patterns. *How can I compete with all Jacob can offer her or with her father's memory? Such good men. Me? I'm only . . .*

Just then, the tips of the fire stretched up and away from him as the outside door opened and shut. A loose knit scarf swathed all but Mollie's glistening eyes as her hunched figure leaned back against the heavy oak door to secure it against the night wind. When she drew the scarf back and stood up straighter, she jumped at the sight of Israel seated by the hearth looking over his shoulder at her.

The reflection of the fire sparked in her tears. Israel had turned to her, but didn't get up, knowing by her wide eyes that his presence had already shocked her. "Didn't mean to startle you," he said. "Jacob asked me to stay tonight to help with whatever the storm might bring." She gave no response. "Are you all right?" he asked. "You've been crying." He stood, but made no move to approach her as much as he ached to wrap her in his arms.

"I . . . I . . . I burned my hand on the stove plate," she stammered wrapping her hand in her loosened scarf as a ruse.

"Is it bad?" Israel asked immediately concerned as he moved to her side and lifted the bundled hand to inspect it.

At his touch, their eyes met and lingered. He gently lifted her hand toward his lips, but at the last second she drew it away and pushed past him.

102

Both struggled to mask their shallow breathing, to avoid facing one another.

"It'll be fine," she said fiddling with the makeshift bandage. "It'll be . . ."

Israel lowered himself to the edge of the crude rope bed by the wall and sighed. "Soon as the weather clears, I'll be leaving, Mollie." He faltered. "I mean leaving the valley. Leaving Waynesburg."

Her heart stopped. *What? Leaving? Where? How? . . .* But she said nothing and held her place.

At her silence, he continued, "Some of my kin moved to Ohio last year. They wrote that the soil's rich and the opportunities many. I love my family, but with 12 brothers and sisters, Papa's hard put to find a place for us all."

Mollie finally turned and gazed at him.

He shook his head and ground his wrists into his thighs to control the intense urge to go to her. "I have to think about the future – a wife – someone to be with. If I stay here, I can think of no one but you, Mollie, and we both know that you and Jacob . . ."

Mollie covered her face with her hands and crumpled to the floor, suddenly sobbing. Again Israel resisted his instinct to go to her. *She's Jacob's, not mine. Not mine,* he repeated in his mind as he kept his place. *But Lord, I want her so much. I . . .*

"Please, Israel. Don't leave me. Please don't go." Mollie lifted her head as she pleaded. "I need you. God help me, I need you so."

In an instant, he dropped to the packed dirt floor and held her to him as she wept into his chest. His mind was racing, but he waited, suppressing his own need to know what had happened until she was ready – able – to tell him. "I'm here, Mollie." He rocked her soothingly. "I'm here. As long as you need me, I won't go."

As much as Israel was mystified, as much as he wanted to know why – for whatever reason they were together, he didn't want this moment to end. He finally felt her full weight fall against him as she calmed. He lifted her chin and whispered. "I love you, Mollie."

She looped her hand around his neck and drew his lips to hers, kissing him delicately but deeply.

"And I love you, Israel. I'll deny it no longer." She nestled against him as they hugged. "This is where I belong." She sighed. "If you'll have me."

"Always, my love. Always."

Elizabeth drew the long-handled bed warmer back and forth between the cold blankets of the bed that she and Mollie would once again share after Elizabeth's long sojourn at Snow Hill. "Morning will come too soon," she said to Mollie. "We've been nearly an hour talking about my time at Snow Hill. I'm so glad I can share my heart with you, and that you understand. But what about you?"

"What do you mean?" asked Mollie pulling her hair into a bun.

Elizabeth drew back the blankets and they both snuggled into the featherbed. "You were so long coming back from the summer kitchen this evening, and since then you haven't been yourself. You left the table so quietly, barely a word. Is anything wrong? Did something happen while I was away?"

Mollie smoothed the coverlet and drew a deep breath. "Much has happened, Elizabeth. Like you, my life is changing so fast that I can barely keep up at times. I need to share *my* heart with *you* now, and pray God you can understand."

They lay down side by side with their sleeping bonnets nested on their pillows. "If not by birth, then by spirit, Mollie, you're my sister. Tell me what's troubling you."

"Israel Baer, Elizabeth," Mollie confessed.

Elizabeth closed her eyes at the revelation as Mollie continued. "Our love has taken root and can't be shaken." Elizabeth listened as Mollie poured out her heart. ". . . so you see, we must go to Ohio and soon, before any more harm is done. We can't let our love hurt the people we care about. We need to spare Jacob, especially, as much as we can. He deserves that much, and more . . ."

Elizabeth, who had listened patiently, grabbed Mollie's hand tightly as tears hung on her cheeks. "I'll miss you more than you know, Mollie. But God's blessing and mine go with you and Israel." Sister Melonia's words filled her head. *'The heart is life's true compass, but sometimes it takes you places you never thought you would go.'*

Mollie returned Elizabeth's squeeze. "Thank you and bless you too, Elizabeth," she said. "Not a word, though, until Israel finds the right time to speak with Jacob. He will as soon as the way's clear for us to travel."

"Not a word," Elizabeth repeated. "God's will be done."

Both women closed their eyes, but sleep did not come easy for either one.

The sparkling snow came and went, a feast for the eyes and less severe than expected. Cate managed to treat Nan, young Daniel and Jane to a half dozen shovelhead sled rides down the long gradual hill just west of the manor before the skiff of powder disappeared. Samuel smiled when he heard their squeals of delight while he was in the barn inspecting the travel worthiness of the metal rimmed wooden wheels of his wagon for the return trip to Cove Forge. *I remember the catch in my stomach flying down that same hill with David, Elizabeth, and Polly,* he thought as he went around the corner to investigate.

Jane was halfway down the slope huddled on her makeshift sled as Cate gave young Daniel a firm push from the top. Jane spun to a stop just a few feet in front of Samuel. She raised her head just as her brother's shovelhead flew up beside her kicking a wave of snow into her face.

"Oh no!" she cried wiping her eyes with the frosted backs of her mittens. "Daniel, why did you . . ."

Samuel scooped her up and laughed. "That's all part of playing in the snow, *Liebchen*."

Young Daniel pounded his sled against the ground to knock off the packed coating it had picked up on his descent. "*Ja, du dummes Mädchen*, a little snow won't hurt you." He grabbed her abandoned sled along with his own and started back up toward Cate who was waving from the crest of the hill. "Let's go again while the snow lasts. Look here comes Nan, now," he pointed at his cousin's sled following the path he had just laid.

Jane wriggled down from Samuel's grasp and started off.

"Enjoy yourselves," Samuel called after them. "Bright and early tomorrow, we leave for home. Only five days 'til Christmas and we need to be with Mama and the little ones by then."

By early January the mill pond had frozen to a slate gray, thick enough to harvest ice to use in the distant warmer months for sweet iced cream and iced-packed cargos of fresh produce destined for distant markets. It was a torturous labor of sawing, hauling, loading, and storing the large, heavy blocks in freezing temperatures.

Israel spread the final layer of straw on the frozen slabs stacked in the icehouse. "Today's work was a fine start on filling this shed again," he said to Jacob, who was checking Siggy's harness after a hard morning's labor.

"I just hope your brother Uriah can fill your shoes. We're surely going to miss you," Jacob said.

"These are pretty sizable boots," replied Israel kicking a nearby hay mound. "But Uriah makes some impressive footprints of his own. He's not quite the ox that my older brother Jesse is, but he carries a sweeter disposition. Takes after me," he quipped. "Jesse is like my papa reborn, a real badger most times. That's why he'll be the best to run the Baer family mill." He brushed the debris from his sleeves and trousers. "Come tomorrow, Uriah will be working with you and I'll be heading west."

"Do you have all you need for the journey?" asked Jacob.

"I think I've planned well enough," he answered. "Only one more thing I need." He hesitated and looked long at Jacob.

"What?" Jacob asked puzzled by Israel's pause.

Israel swallowed hard. "I need to tell you . . . to tell you that . . ." He closed his eyes. ". . . that Mollie's coming with me. She's at the wagon waiting for me now."

Jacob froze, then dropped his gaze and turned his back. A heavy silence fell between them as he absorbed the news. Israel waited for a response. Unable to endure the prolonged quiet, Israel finally spoke. "You've every right to hate me, Jacob. I know how much you care for Mollie." Jacob removed his hat and wiped his brow, still silent.

Israel inched a step closer. "You need to know that I love Mollie." He noticed Jacob's back and shoulders tighten. "We'll not be gone half a day before we're properly married – in Hager's-town. I'll be good to her, Jacob. She couldn't bring herself to tell you. I hate doing it myself. We both . . ."

"Enough," Jacob pronounced stepping away from Israel. "No more." He turned. "I waited – watched – prayed each night – that she could come to love me. Though I've never had a woman look at me with love, I knew I'd recognize it when it happened, just as I knew it was only deep respect and concern I saw in Mollie's eyes."

He gazed at Israel. "How can I hate you for loving Mollie when I love her too? How can I blame the woman I love for being honest with me?" His voice cracked and eyes glazed. "I think I knew this day was coming." He put on his hat, reached into his small waist pocket and drew out something that he clutched in his hand.

"What can I . . . ?" Israel began, desperate to offer Jacob some relief. But, Jacob held up his palm to silence him and sat on the edge of the drag sled as Siggy pawed the ground sensing the unease.

"A minute," whispered Jacob. "Be still and let me think, just a minute." In his lap, he cradled his fist with his other hand and rolled whatever he held over and over, caressing it, lost in thought.

Israel found a seat on a low, hay strewn ice stack. *What's he holding? What's he thinking?* He felt his heart pumping in his ears, his throat thickening in this eternity of waiting. *Talk to me, Jacob. Tell me something – anything.*

 As if reading Israel's thoughts, Jacob finally stood. He took hold of Israel's arm and pulled it toward him. "Open your hand, Israel." Israel rotated his wrist and uncurled his calloused fingers. Jacob achingly poured a delicate silver locket and chain from his hand into Jacob's. "It belonged to Ephraim. I found it under some empty sacks at the mill weeks after the accident. He told me once that it belonged to his wife, Mollie's mother. Not right that I keep it now. It was to be part of my proposal to Mollie as soon as I won her heart."

"Jacob, I can't," Israel pleaded.

Jacob closed Israel's fingers over the treasure. "You must. You must tell Mollie that this is her Da's blessing. And . . ." He gasped. ". . . and . . ." He clamped his hand over his mouth to suppress a sob as his face twisted in pain. He bent over and backed away stepping blindly until he bumped into the log wall of the shed behind him. ". . . and mine."

He fled leaving Israel stunned. "Dear God, how could we do this?" He stared at the locket and all it meant. "But how could we not?"

-11-

The Love Feast

Rebecca lay quietly in bed as the latch clicked on the bedroom door. The faint chirp of an early spring cricket echoed just outside the open window as she listened carefully for any sign that Cate had awakened from her deep sleep on the nearby cot. *After all that work in the fields and the four-square garden, we should all be sleeping like her*, she thought. *Susan's been tossing all night – and now she's gone. Something's wrong and I'm gonna find out what.* She eased out from the covers and picked her way though the gray shadows out into the hall in search of her older sister.

Susan sat on the stirring stool by the smoldering hearth in the deserted kitchen with her hands wrapped around a tin cup of spring water she had drawn from the sink pump. Rebecca paused in the doorway to watch her for some clue to her mood. Finding nothing more distinctive than deep thought on Susan's dimly lit face, Rebecca finally spoke. "What is it, Susan? What has you awake at this hour?"

Susan jumped slightly and sighed. "I didn't mean to disturb you, Rebecca." She drained the cup and put it on the floor.

"I was never really asleep. You were squirming like a newborn colt most of the night. Can you tell me what's bothering you? I'll not tell a soul. You know that." Rebecca lowered herself to the rug beside her.

After a few seconds, Susan confessed. "It's the reconciliation. You know, we're to set things right in our heart and with others before the foot washing and Communion at the Love Feast tomorrow."

"That's not an easy task for anyone, but not so much as to keep us awake." She took Susan's hand. "I know you only need to share your fears with the Lord," she said. "But it might help to talk it out. Thoughts get too cloudy and confusing when we keep them to ourselves."

Susan bowed her head and took Rebecca's hand in both of hers. "It's about Henry."

In spite of her sister's distress, Rebecca couldn't help but smile. "Henry? But he loves you, Susan. Everyone can see that."

"Does he?" Susan blurted louder than she intended. Searching the room to make sure no one else had heard, she lowered her voice and repeated, "Does he really, Rebecca?" She stood and moved away staring at the crescent moon through the back window. "Has he told *you* that, because he certainly hasn't told *me*?" Tears pooled in her eyes.

"I'm sorry, Susan. I didn't know. It's just so obvious."

"It feels so when we're together. But he's not said as much, so neither can I. When I feel the warm spring soil in the garden, all I can think about is planting my celery – being his wife. Every day it doesn't happen, I'm more frightened it won't. That I'm wrong about him. That . . . that . . ." She started to cry. "How can I reconcile that? How can I say anything to him?"

Rebecca marched up beside her, crossed her arms over her chest and harrumphed. "Why do the *men* have to say it first? Why do *we* have to wait for *them*? That's what I'd like to know. "

"Oh, I couldn't go first!" Susan whispered. "What if he didn't say it back? What if I told him I loved him and he said nothing?" She began to pant. "Then he might leave. I'd never be with him again."

Rebecca hugged her. "Calm down, *Schwester*. Henry's not going anywhere. I don't know how you can resolve this with him right now. The way things are, you need to leave it to God and let that be reconciliation enough until Henry gets a voice."

"It's so hard, Rebecca. I'm so scared. When I see the sadness of a lost love in Jacob's eyes, his loneliness, it frightens me so."

"Come to bed now. Let the world keep spinning instead of your head. You'll have the brotherly love of the entire congregation at the Love Feast tomorrow to support you. Henry's can wait for now."

"I'm so glad we've taken the wagon instead of two buggies," said Cate lifting her face to the morning sun. "Would be a shame to miss this beautiful view."

"*Ja. Ich stimme zu,*" squealed Nan. "I love the breeze against my cheeks."

Daniel and Catherine seated on the driver's bench above swayed in tandem with their daughters as the wagon rocked over the uneven path of the final approach to Snow Hill. When Cate's enthusiasm prompted no response from her older sisters, Catherine turned to investigate. Susan, Rebecca and Elizabeth wore blank expressions, lost in serious thought. *A somber lot for such a day*, she pondered. *Especially Elizabeth. Strange. She should be looking forward to seeing her Snow Hill friends again . . . I wonder . . .*

Their quiet wasn't lost on Cate, either. She eyed her subdued traveling companions. "Why so glum? How can you resist this glorious day?" The three white bonnets continued their rhythmic bobbing, her sisters giving no sign of having heard her questions. They were oblivious to her, their minds full of other concerns.

Susan stared blankly aheaded. *Henry, will you find the words today? Will he, Lord?*

Rebecca gave Susan's hand a reassuring squeeze thinking, *Clear Henry from your mind, Susan. Love the Lord, today.*

 Elizabeth folded her hands in her lap. *David, will I know more today of what your looks were saying? Can we really speak of it?*

Cate frowned at them and leaned out the back of the wagon. "Jacob! David!" she called to her brothers following closely behind on Maggie and Elsie. "Have you ever seen a prettier day?" She lifted her hands to the dazzling sky.

Jacob surveyed the countryside, tipped his head as if considering, then replied, "Spring's ablaze, for sure, Cate. Thank you for giving it song as well."

"A fine day surely," David agreed. Then he turned to Jacob and added softly, "Though I could do without such antics as Cate's. I'm sure you've had enough of women as well."

"You know, David. I've come to believe we all take in the world in our own way, as God wills it. When the world brings us burdens, He offers other blessings – like Cate – to lift us up."

Henry Reighart reigned in his horse as he peered across Quincy Road toward Snow Hill. George Smith pulled his roan up alongside. "Look here, Henry," he said.

Henry shifted toward him. "What?"

George squinted and leaned his face to within inches of Henry's nose. "Your eyes are open, I see."

"Yes," groused Henry pulling back and blinking at the intrusion.

"Now," George insisted coming close again, "open your mouth."

Henry yanked his horse away from George. "Get away. You gone daft?"

George spurred his roan into the other horse's flank ignoring Henry's resistance. "I said, 'open your mouth.'"

"You *have* lost your mind," Henry barked. "Back off!"

"That's possible, I suppose, but even if I've lost my *mind*, I need to see if you've lost your *tongue*," said George.

Henry shook his head in frustration and glared at his friend.

"Give me those *looks* all you want," said George. "Just make sure you give *Fräulein* Susan some *words* today with that tongue I just spied. And I mean some *real* words."

"Watch it!" Henry snapped as his cheeks colored. "That's not for you to judge. It's not as easy as you might think to take such a risk."

"*Life* is a risk, *mein Freund.* Nearly every day at the forge someone is hurt – or dies. And not just the workers. Last week we buried two young, once healthy, women. One from pneumonia and the other from snakebite." George paused to soften his tone. "All I'm saying is, if you love your Susan, tell her. Don't be wasting this precious time." He smiled. "Besides, I've seen how she looks at you. You won't be disappointed with her response."

Henry adjusted his hat and squared his shoulders. "Today *is* all about reconciliation. You might be right, George." Then he grinned and returned George's earlier gesture meeting him nose to nose. "For once." He laughed and spurred his horse down the road with George in pursuit.

The soft hills of new yellow-green grass surrounding the red brick common building and the churning mill of Snow Hill had been humming with preparations for the expected crowd since near dawn the day before. Two large butchering kettles brimming with the traditional beef and bread *Supp* for the Agape meal sat bubbling on open flames. Temporary tables and seating for the feast appeared in every available level area still wet and sparkling with early morning dew.

Basins and stacks of folded linen cloths were readied at the front of the common worship area for the foot washing, a reenactment of Jesus' humble act of washing His disciples' feet at the Passover meal the evening before His crucifixion. Baskets of unleavened bread and small glasses of grape juice were housed in the large sideboard of the cloister's large kitchen. They would accompany the solemn Communion to conclude the ceremonies for the day. The elements were reminiscent of the wine and bread, symbolic of His flesh and blood, that Jesus and His followers had shared before His death.

Peter Lehman, the Order's revered patriarch, clapped Andrew Fahnestock, a longstanding mainstay of the cloister, on the back as they exited the impressive community barn. "A miraculous job, Brother Andrew. The ground has barely settled on the graves of those poor suffering animals and our new herd is already flourishing."

"Thanks to the brotherhood in Ephrata and generous neighbors like the Royers and the Cochrans and others who gave us aid in our trials," said Andrew stroking his long white beard as he leaned on his heavy wooden staff. "My nephew Thomas has done an outstanding job handling this crisis. Fortunate that the Lord has led him our way."

"How fortunate that our Watch Night Love Feast falls on a Friday, so that neither our Sabbath nor the Sabbath of our German Baptist Brethren is compromised," said Peter. "We can *all* participate today and our Easter services that follow will be even more joyous for the unity we'll have with our friends."

"The first arrivals will soon be here," said Andrew scanning the horizon for evidence of approaching wagons or horses. "Look, the Royers are at the rise. No doubt Elizabeth, their eldest, is anxious to find out how their cows have been doing since she brought them to us last November. Thomas told me she had quite an affection for the animals."

"As I recall she and Melonia became close friends during that time together. I'll go to the kitchen and let our sister know Elizabeth's here," said Peter.

"Best I see to any last minute needs." Andrew drew in a deep breath. "Ahhh, Peter. The spirit is strong today. May we be worthy of the Lord's blessings."

"This day and always." Peter closed his eyes and bowed his head briefly, then inhaled, mirroring Andrew's earlier action, and smiled. *"Gott ist gut – Gott ist immer gut."* Now, let's begin this joyful work of our Father."

 "Looks like you've gotten very comfortable here, Elsa," said Elizabth admiring the well-kept condition of the familiar Snow Hill stable as she scratched the area between the cow's shorthorns just the way she knew Elsa liked. Fresh straw lined each of the stalls and all the manure had been swept into the barn's gutters. She noticed the silky tuft at the tip of Elsa's swishing tail. "They've even cleaned and combed your tail." The animal shook its head and large neck and gazed at Elizabeth with glassy brown eyes.

"She's been giving fine milk every day for months. A sure sign she's contented," came a soothing, equally familiar voice.

Elizabeth spun around. "Melonia!" She dashed to the frail, contorted lady clad in the plain garb of the sisterhood, but tempered the huge hug she felt like giving her old friend to a gentle embrace. "I was just comng to look for you."

"Pastor Lehman saw you arrive and remembered the friendship we share. I started for the barn the moment . . ." She paused gasping for breath. ". . . the moment he told me." She put her hand to her chest. "How are . . ." Her breathing became more labored.

Elizabeth quickly grabbed a milking stool and helped Melonia sit down. "I'm fine," said Elizabeth, "but I can see *you* aren't well. May I get you some water? Should I call someone to help?" Elizabeth patted Melonia's twisted hands resting on her knees.

"No, no," Melonia wheezed softly. "Just a short rest." She drew some slow, easier breaths. "This spell will soon pass."

Elizabeth sat on the barn floor at her feet. "Have you been ill?"

Melonia gently lifted Elizabeth's chin. "No child. The same disease that bends my bones now steals my breath as well. Nothing to be done but what God wills." After a few shallow pants, she continued slowly. "Your dear face is the best remedy I know. Now, tell me about yourself. What's happened since we were last together? I often think of you when I go to the prayer room."

Elizabeth faltered. "I . . . we . . . I can't think what to say. Seeing you so weak has taken my words."

"There, now. No hurry. Just be sure to save some words for *Herr* Good." She drew some short breaths. "He comes to visit your cows every day he's here, and not for their sweet milk, I think, but for . . ." She smiled and breathed deeply. ". . . for sweet memories of you."

Elizabeth blushed.

Leather boots and shoes of every size and condition stuffed with musky rolled stockings were tucked under benches or lined up along the wall of the small room adjacent to the worship hall. The women arranged their long skirts modestly to conceal their bare feet as best they could and secured small linen towels around their waists with strings. A solemn reverence settled on their faces. One by one they filed out and took their places on the left side of the worship hall.

A flock of black hats hung on wooden pegs just inside the door. The men, barefoot as well, waited prayerfully on the right side of the room with empty boots tucked under the hard oak benches where they sat.

Basins of water rested on the floor at the outer end of each row of both sections. At the prompting of Pastor Lehman, the evocative tones of a capella singing began and would continue throughout the foot washing – a powerful sign of both servitude and love.

"*Lobt Gott ihr Christian all zu gleich,*" the congregation sang.

Ja, thought Elizabeth, '*Let all together praise our God.*'

Everyone present took their turn, placing each foot, one by one, in the water to be washed and dried in turn by a fellow member. The two would then embrace with a holy kiss and greeting, 'God bless you, Sister' or 'God bless you, Brother.'
Then the roles were exchanged, and so it would proceed until all had participated. The unspoken prayers were as varied as the needs of

each individual, but the oneness with God and the community of believers was shared by all.

With minds refreshed by reconciliation and spirits renewed by the emotional foot washing service, the celebrants emerged from the building, once again in stockings and boots, to the sunbathed day and the lively fellowship of food and celebration.

Rebecca cradled her bowl of sloshing hot bean soup as she wove her way through the crowd to a place next to Susan at the family table near the corner of a field striped by fresh, broad-leafed shoots of corn. Cate and Nan sat opposite them with a space between already vacated by Elizabeth who had excused herself to talk with the other sisters she had come to know in her time there.

As Rebecca slurped her first taste from the small wooden scoop, a burst of deep laughter emerged above the rumble of the crowd near a small copse of trees toward the barn. "Does that laugh sound familiar to you?" asked Susan wiping her mouth and craning her head in the direction of the outburst.

The other girls paused to listen when the hearty chuckle rang out again. "That's Jacob!" cried Nan, astonished by her brother's laughter.

"You're right," Rebecca agreed. "It's been so long since we've heard his laugh, I nearly forgot how sweet it sounds." She followed Susan's smiling gaze. Soon the ends of her mouth curled up too when she discovered that Jacob's companions, the friends who had awakened his dormant good cheer, were Henry Reighart and George Smith.

As if he felt their stares, Henry raised his head in the girls' direction. Like opposite magnetic poles, his eyes connected with Susan's. The slice of sweet nut bread she was holding dropped onto the table and Cate grabbed it. "Whatever's caught Susan's attention must be even more tempting than this delicious raisin stollen," she teased. Then she noticed Rebecca's expression. "And Rebecca's got a taste of it, too." Cate spun around in time to see Henry in the distance. He nodded slightly in Susan's direction and lifted his brows indicating a quieter patch of grass by the edge of the nearby mill race.

Unaware her silent exchange with Henry had been observed, Susan said, "Since most everyone's been served, think I'll get another helping of the *Supp*." Her deception was foiled when she rose and walked away leaving her bowl on the table.

Cate pointed at the empty dish and giggled. "Wonder if Susan's gonna eat right from the serving ladle?" She scrunched her shoulders. "Or better yet, maybe she'll borrow *Henry's* bowl." She then whispered something to Nan who began to titter as well.

"Hush up and mind your own business, you two nosy bugs," scolded Rebecca. "There's plenty else to do here today. Leave Susan be."

Susan made a wide circle past the depleted kettles, winding her way behind the mill and coming round the far corner to the narrow run of the gently lapping water of the mill run where Henry waited under a shade tree.

"Hello, Susan," he said making it appear to be a chance meeting to anyone who might be watching or within hearing distance.

"Oh, hello, Henry," she answered feigning surprise. "Fine day we're having."

"*Ja, sehr gut*," he agreed. Then he pointed behind the mill. "Is that a fox running up the rise? They've been losing chickens here lately. Best check it out." He brushed past her behind the structure out of sight.

Susan lingered a short while, her heart racing, as she casually scanned the crowd for witnesses. Seeing none, she slipped behind the mill as well. *Gott im Himmel, what am I doing?* she fretted to herself as she started up the hill.

"I love you, Susan," came a voice behind her.

She stopped short and closed her eyes. *Danke, mein Gott.* She felt a hand on her shoulder. Holding her breath, she turned to face him.

Henry took her hand. "Susan, I love you with all my heart."

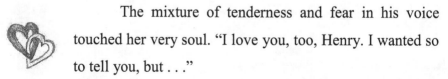 The mixture of tenderness and fear in his voice touched her very soul. "I love you, too, Henry. I wanted so to tell you, but . . ."

He lifted her chin and kissed her. They remained so for a time. Then he moved back and they gazed at each other clasping their hands between them. "I spoke with your papa earlier today. With his and God's blessing, will you be my wife?"

"Yes!" she declared. She flung her arms around him knocking him off balance. They clung to each other as they fell backwards and hit the ground becoming a tangled mass of arms and legs as they tumbled down the hill and rolled into the mill's brick wall.

Laughing and shushing each other at the same time, afraid of being discovered, they finally nestled together in a cushion of fragrant soapwort along the stone foundation, stealing what they knew could be only a precious few moments together.

Atop the horizon on a hill south of the gathering, solitary against the backdrop of blank sky, stood a lone tree. Branches outstretched, it stood watch over Earth while reaching toward Heaven. The tree may have been planted to mark the boundary of a field, but Elizabeth had deemed it *her* witness tree months earlier. Now spring had urged life into the once bare limbs. She studied its feathered arms brushing the scattered white clouds as she trod up the slate-ridged slope toward the comfort of its canopy. *So like me,* she considered. *Alone. Drawn to*

Heaven, but rooted in the earth. Drinking in the sacred gifts of God, but more akin to the world, to my heart . . . to . . .

"*Fräulein* Elizabeth." David Good stepped out from behind the sturdy girth of the solid white oak, the gentleness in his eyes belying the power of his frame. "I've been praying you would come."

She froze, unable to respond.

"I didn't mean to startle you. I stood behind the tree because I wanted you to come of your own accord. I was afraid my being here might somehow frighten you away, but I needed to speak to you – alone. I remembered your coming here last fall – the peace you found here. I've been praying the Lord would lead you here today . . . to me."

The pulse of the landscape moved on to the next measure. Most serving pots and crocks were down to crumbs and dregs. The general cleanup tasks hastened the tempo as the afternoon sun continued its decline. The elements for the impending Communion feast had been moved to the worship center in preparation for the final ceremony to take place before all the visitors would depart.

Catherine wedged the small empty pickle crock and pan that they had emptied of creamed turnips into her reed basket. "Nan, run over to the sweets table and gather up our pie tins. Mind you watch out for the bees. They've been hovering around the cider kegs and sugars all day."

"Yes, Mama," she said dashing away.

Daniel planted his elbows on the table and propped his chin on his hands. "I suppose I should go find David and Jacob. Soon time for Communion."

Rebecca stacked the family's nine redware bowls in the basket and wrapped a cloth around them for traveling. As she tucked the wooden spoons in beside them, she remarked, "Seems to be one missing."

"And I seem to have *two* daughters missing," Catherine said glancing left and right. "Cate's over by the big sycamore playing on the rope swings, but have you seen Elizabeth or Susan?"

"Oh, that reminds me, Catherine," said Daniel before Rebecca could answer. "Henry Reighart had a word with me earlier today when the men gathered before the foot washing. You and I will speak of it this evening."

Catherine's eyes widened and Rebecca stifled a gasp as Daniel made a quick departure, not anxious for further discussion.

"Oh Mama, I think Susan might soon be in search of some celery seed," whispered Rebecca.

"We'll know quick enough. Say nothing 'til we know for sure," Catherine warned her, unable to keep from smiling. "Now where are those girls?"

Young Benjamin Sprecht hoisted one of the ten-foot planks from the sawhorses of the makeshift table onto his shoulder. "This is the last of the lot for the first group," he said beginning another of what would be many trips to the barn to store the wood. He firmed up his two-handed hold on the precariously balanced board as he passed the stand of cider kegs. Suddenly, an aggressive bee zoomed directly at his face, buzzing inches from his nose. Instinctively, Benjamin whipped his head to the side, his shoulders following suit. With this action, the heavy plank started cutting a wide swath in front and behind him, but abruptly stopped with a sickening thud. Benjamin cringed, knowing immediately what had happened.

"Cate!" Catherine's scream echoed across the field as she saw the end of the board smash into her daughter's head throwing her violently to the ground.

By the witness tree, Elizabeth had just found her voice. "David, you need not have hidden yourself from me, I . . ."

At Catherine's shriek from below, Elizabeth spun around. The rush of the crowd drew her focus to the small body lying on the ground. David Good saw the crumpled figure as well and hurried to

Elizabeth's side. They shared a look of painful disbelief and ran toward the scene.

The air of calamity struck Susan and Henry as they came around the side of the mill. Henry grabbed hold of Wilhelm Knepper who was racing toward the frantic crowd. "What's happened, Brother?" Henry asked.

"A child's been hurt. Struck hard and unconscious," he answered. Then he noticed Susan and froze. "I think it was *seiner Mutter* who cried out," he mumbled.

"*Lieber Gott*," Susan wailed.

-11-

Uncertain Days

Brown trails of caked mud clung to the sides of Cate's swollen forehead where blood had seeped out from under the initial makeshift bandage. One of the Snow Hill sisters prepared a fresh dressing as Catherine held her daughter's limp hand and stroked the pink youthful skin with her fingers, twisted and veined with age. *Lord, you spared her once when the rattlesnake struck. Please, don't take her from us yet – not yet.*

Cate's white cap rested atop the woven coverlet that kept off the chill of approaching evening. She lay on a small bed in the sisters' wing where Pastor Lehman had told Jacob to carry her. He had been the first to reach his mother's side after her scream rang out across the field hours earlier.

Only Cate's slow, shallow breathing denied her death. The swelling extended from the huge knot above her left eye through her cheeks and upper lip tinging her distorted face a ghastly grayish blue.

Sister Zenobia gently removed the old poultice to re-dress Cate's wound. "The swelling's considerable because the cut didn't bleed much." Along the ridge of the point of impact was a frayed line of deep purple dried blood. She gently cleaned the injury with a damp linen cloth and applied the fresh ointment securing the pack with a narrow length of cloth. Then she took Catherine's hands in hers. "There are no broken bones, no bleeding from her ears, nose, or eyes. She breathes easily and evenly." Reading the anguish on Catherine's face, Sister Zenobia added, "These are all *good* signs, *Frau* Royer. She will wake when the trauma in her head has settled. It could be today, or next week – in God's time. We'll know more then."

"Excuse me, Sister Zenobia." Thomas Fahnestock's frame stood silhouetted in the narrow doorway. "Pastor Lehman has sent me with the Communion elements for you and *Frau* Royer." He extended a plate covered with a cloth and a small glass of grape juice. "He also sends word that *Fräulein* Cate has been remembered in all of our prayers at the service."

Catherine's focus on Cate never wavered. Sister Zenobia took the young man's offering. "*Danke*," she whispered. "I'm not sure *Frau* Royer heard you, but I'll let her know and we'll partake together."

Thomas shook his head and backed out the door.

Hours later, Catherine sat in the bed of the family wagon at the top of the featherbed offered by the Snow Hill sisterhood. She made a nest in her lap and Daniel lowered Cate's body gently in place with Catherine cradling her head. The other girls wedged themselves alongside their sister to help absorb the jostling on the trip home.

As Peter Lehman and *Herr* Hess approached, Daniel climbed out of the wagon. "*Danke,*" he said as they shared a parting kiss of brotherhood. "We are much in your debt."

"Not at all, Brother," said Pastor Lehman. "*Gott ist mit Ihnen.*"

Daniel pushed the remaining circles of ragged sausage around his plate. Throughout the evening meal he had stolen glances at Catherine's vacant seat at the opposite end of the table.

The others around the table were noticeably quieter than usual. The ten-day absence from the dinner table of their mother and Cate, the family's tonic of good cheer, was taking its toll – on Daniel most of all. Elizabeth hazarded breaking the silence, fearful of Daniel's obvious foul humor. "May I be excused, Papa – to take supper to Mama?"

"It's time she returned to the table." He tossed his fork in frustration. "One of you girls can attend Cate and call us if she wakes."

"*When* she wakes," Rebecca corrected abruptly, then withered under her father's stern expression. "*Es ist traurig*, Papa. But I *have* to believe she *will* wake, or I can't stand it."

"So we all hope and pray," added Susan coming to her sister's aid.

Nan's lower lip began to quiver and her eyes glistened with tears.

"Clear the table," Daniel ordered pushing away from his place. "Devotions in one hour."

David rose without comment and followed his father out of the room.

After a pause to ensure they were gone, Jacob leaned into the table and explained to his sisters, "Papa's anger hides his concern. He struggles with softness. His responsibilities demand a hardness that often seems cruel. Don't judge too harshly or be offended too easily. No one will rejoice more than Papa when Cate recovers."

As the tension drained from the room, Elizabeth began to fill a plate from what remained in the serving dishes. Nan made her way to Jacob's side and wrapped her arms around his neck. He lifted her to his lap and she nestled her head into his chest. Susan began stacking the tableware as Rebecca swept the scattered crumbs into the palm of her hand and tossed them in the empty basket that once held warm, yellow fingers of corn pone.

Elizabeth balanced the plate of victuals and tankard of cider as she nudged the bedroom door open with her hip. "Oh!" she cried as Mukki sped in behind her unexpectedly, catching her skirt and challenging her footing. She scowled at the dog as Catherine turned in the chair beside the bed to investigate. "What are you doing up here, Mukki? You know better than to . . ."

But the usually placid dog paid no heed and began licking Cate's hand while her tail thumped an excited rhythm against Catherine's skirt and the side of the bed.

"Mukki?" mumbled Cate as her long idle eyelids began to flutter.

The dog barked a response as Catherine leapt to her feet and grasped Cate's shoulders searching for recognition on her daughter's face. "Cate?" she said.

Their eyes met and the corners of Cate's mouth moved ever so slightly. "Mama?"

Elizabeth froze, nearly dropping the plate of food. Catherine turned her head to confirm the answer to their ardent prayers. "Tell your Papa we'll hear devotions up here with Cate tonight," she said, tears streaming down her cheeks. She turned back to Cate and they smiled again. "We – *all* of us – will give thanks *together* this evening."

Cate's prolonged coma had caused the muscles of her young limbs to atrophy, but every day she regained more of her strength and usual spark. Susan was her companion on her first excursion outside the house. With small tin pails looped through the apron ties around their waists, they strolled along the west bank of the Antietam's roiling spring rush in search of wild strawberries.

"They've just started to ripen," Susan explained. "And the early rain has thickened the vines and leaves. Hard to spy those tiny red spots."

Cate squinted. "Looks like a sprinkling just ahead down the slope." She picked up her pace and began sidestepping toward the berries. Susan resisted the urge to take her arm, not wanting to be overprotective, anxious for Cate to regain her self-confidence.

Susan spotted more fruit next to the patch Cate was working and knelt beside her. "On the way back to the house we'll have to check my new celery bed." She paused her picking to catch Cate's response.

Cate plunked one and then another speckled berry into her pail before she stopped to consider the significance of Susan's statement. Her mouth dropped open and she stared hard at her older sister. Susan was grinning broadly and nodded her head.

Cate threw her arms around Susan. "Where? When?" asked Cate.

"At the Love Feast. Just before your accident."

"Well," Cate laughed. "I'm not sure yet if that old board knocked any sense into *my* head, but something surely did the job for Henry Reighart."

-13-

A Sultry Summer

The strong midday July sun bleached the sky and wrinkled the countryside. Green leaves and stalks drooped with the dense humidity of an uncommonly rainy summer. Plump seeded heads of the stand of rye on the western horizon sagged awaiting the first harvest of the season. White lime dust lined every crevice of the four-square garden to ward off bugs and pestilence.

"Only the weeds welcome this awful heat," said Susan kneeling on the tanbarked path as she pulled a fistful of flat-leafed *Greidel* from the raised bed jammed with heavily laden wax bean vines.

"A little breeze would feel heavenly," whined Nan as she dumped an apron load of plump pea pods into the large gathering basket by the whitewashed gate.

"But a wind might stir up the stink of the tannery. I'd just as soon sweat as smell that," Cate reminded her sitting back on her heels by the bed of mint. "Mama will need lots of this to add to the spring water and cider for the workers' noon meal." She added a handful of deep green feathery sprigs to the small sack dangling from her waist and wiped the rivulets of perspiration from her forehead with the back of her hand. "It's so hot that . . ."

"I'm sure those poor families at Old Forge are *truly* suffering with the added heat of those dreadful furnaces and charcoaling mounds," Rebecca interrupted.

"You're right," said Susan. "We really shouldn't complain so much, but look." She pointed toward the southwest sky. "Maybe the heavens are going to send all of us some relief." Masses of ominous dark gray thunderheads were rolling up over the roof of the distant barn. The air was suddenly distinctly cooler as the hollow rumble of thunder muffled all other noise. "It's coming in really fast. Better grab our things and get inside. *"Schnell!"*

In a flurry the four girls scooped up their tools and gatherings and dashed toward the summer kitchen, the wind of the impending storm flapping the brims of their gardening hats and twisting their skirts. One after another they leapt over the large puddle in front of the hog pen left by earlier downpours and ducked under the doorway. They fell in a heap on the floor.

Catherine turned away from the large cast iron skillet simmering with fried sausages and onions on the 10-plate stove. "Best you girls move in further – make way for the workers." She tipped her head in the direction of Elizabeth who had just put two large pitchers on the long table where the men would eat. "Elizabeth, ring the dinner bell before the thunder drowns it out or the men get drenched."

Plump raindrops pelted the roof as the workers had their fill of meat and bread and relished some long drafts of mint-flavored drinks. After nearly half an hour, the tempo of the squall slowed to a moderate sprinkle.

"Guess this storm's causing problems at the tannery," said Uriah Baer staring at the three empty spaces across the table from him. "If those rendering vats overflow or the creek rises enough to flood them, there could be some real damage."

"You're right," agreed Jacob pushing away his empty bowl. "It'll be good to see David and his workers here with some news."

"From your mouth to God's ear," said David appearing at the door as he caught the end of Jacob's comment. His beard was lacquered with rain and the soaked brim of his dark hat hung lower than usual over his deep-set eyes. "Was close. Rain came within inches of flooding out the first two pits nearest the stream, but everything's still fine." He hung his dripping hat on a peg and sat at the table as two drenched men behind him did the same. "Let's pray the skies stay clear for at least a few days 'til the ground drains and dries."

Daniel appeared at the door sweeping first one sleeve and then the other free of rain. "And to think just last summer, we were praying for relief from the drought," he said. "If nothing else, my 60 years have taught me that with the weather, the best we can do is wait, watch for signs and deal with whatever each new year brings."

The summer day was drawing toward late afternoon.

"Hannah, take these loaves of pumpernickel home for your family when you finish today." Catherine wiped her hands on her apron as 11-year-old *Fräulein* Mentzer scrubbed the hardwood floor of the Royer dining room.

"*Danke, Frau* Royer," she said swishing the boar bristle brush around in the oaken bucket of cloudy, lye-soaped water. "Papa loves dark bread."

"This summer humidity grows mold on bread faster than hummingbirds beat their wings. Make sure it's part of tonight's supper or tomorrow's breakfast," Catherine advised as she looked out the back window to investigate the giggling that caught her ear. She smiled at the scene. Nan and Hannah's younger sister, Naomi, held

the four corners of a newly laundered blanket they had unfastened from the clothesline. They pumped their arms up and down propelling a pair of bundled socks in the middle of the blanket high in the air as the blanket ballooned up and catching it when it fell. *The Mentzers are good neighbors. Wonderful playmates for Nan and a welcome help around the house. I know their family needs the extra money,* Catherine mused. *Samuel and Sarah would be pleased to know such a fine family's living in their old cabin. I must write them about it this evening.*

Henry and George's horses loped lazily down the muddy road from Old Forge toward Mentzer Gap Road and Waynesburg beyond. As they made their way south, the hot muggy air began to clear leaving behind the smoke and fine ash of the furnaces. "Glad you've determined to stay with us for Sunday Meeting instead of making the trek over the mountain to your family," said Henry.

"I thank you for the invitation and so does Ranger," said George patting his horse's damp neck. "The fewer hills he has to carry me over, the better he likes it." He glanced up the rise to his left as they neared the turn to town. "That's fine brickwork on Ironmaster Beitsel's new mansion. Looks like you masons are nearly finished."

"No more than a month `til they can move in, I'd guess," Henry said.

"Any talk of what'll be done with their old home?" George asked.

143

"Haven't heard. Why?"

"Just wondered," George answered.

"You're a man who does more than 'wonder,'" said Henry eying his companion. "What's rattlin' round in that brain of yours?"

George pulled his reins and turned back toward Old Forge to get a look at the ironmaster's current house some distance behind the new structure. "I was thinking that it might be a school for the forge workers' children."

"A school?"

"Way I see it, there's not much I can do to help their parents," George explained. "They're living hand-to-mouth, not able to save much of anything and at the mercy of those more educated. They'll have a hard time finding a better way of life. Most of them can't read or write. I spend a lot of my time helping them with letters home and notices from the company. The furnace work's too hard for the younger ones and they have almost no land to garden, so they have the time for schooling."

"And, like my papa has said *many* times, 'Idle hands are the Devil's workshop,'" Henry added.

"And the Devil doesn't need any more help than he already has at the forge. Nobody works harder than those men, but they can be a wild lot – more stubborn and independent than ornery mules. Got short fuses, too." George brushed beads of sweat from his upper lip. "This heat only makes pots boil faster."

Henry squinted at the sun wavering on the western slopes. "Well, the worst of this day's passed. We'll have a couple of easier hours after supper back home. Maybe even a cool splash in the creek before the mosquitoes take over."

"I think some of them are as big as the bats that are swarming after them this year, what with all the rain. I've got some welts the size of cherries." George scratched the back of his neck.

The two men continued down the deeply rutted road. "So, how are the wedding plans going?" asked George. "Early November, right?"

"The first Thursday. Can't come too soon." Henry smiled. "Still time to add another couple. There's enough celery in Susan's garden to share with Rebecca."

George stiffened, then shrugged weakly. "I *do* look forward to seeing *Fräulein* Rebecca at Sunday Meeting, but we've not had much time together. She's a hard one to read. She doesn't seem *dis*pleased when she sees me, but that might be just my wishful thinking." He studied Henry's reaction for some clue as to his opinion.

Henry sensed George's probing. "Only one way to find out, as I see it."

"Have Susan ask her?" George suggested with obvious sarcasm.

"Only if *you* suggest that to Susan – not me." Henry tilted his head at George.

George shrugged. "Truly, Brother. Rebecca's a beauty to my eyes, but more importantly, her spirit moves her to act – to help – to make a difference." He sat up straighter and wide-eyed, his face aglow. "I know she's only 16, but she doesn't hesitate to say exactly what's on her mind. It's that spark that I truly . . ." Then he caught himself and slumped back shaking his head again.

Henry slapped him on the back. "Don't be so glum, Brother. Wasn't that long ago, I remember, you told me to 'find my tongue.' Turns out that was excellent advice. Why don't you take it yourself?"

George spurred Ranger and called back over his shoulder. "Can't wait to feel that cool creek water."

Sunday morning birthed a blessedly crisp, clear blue sky. A cottony soft breeze wound through lightened tree branches and lifted window curtains that had hung limply in the previous days' heat. Images sharpened on the distant horizons and the scent of sweet honeysuckle boosted everyone's spirits.

Easy laughter and friendly conversation abounded as the horses and buggies of the neighboring families of the Brethren gathered at the Reighart farm. As with every Sunday Meeting that had come before, all those present came together in the barn that served as their sanctuary. Men and women, on their respective sides, sat for three to four hours of communal worship and prayer followed by the fellowship meal. After the services, the congregation filed out and milled around making their way to family groups for the feast.

"My family's table is over there," Henry told George pointing at a space close to the two-story stone farmhouse. "Feel free to join them or stay with these fellows, if you like. I'm going to sit by Susan at the Royers' table."

"*Danke*. I'll meet you later," said George, standing with a small group of single young men he had met through his acquaintance with Henry.

"*Gut*," said Henry. "Maybe you'll be able to find something sweeter than this bunch by then – and I don't mean the shoo fly pie." He winked at his friend as he left.

"Do my best," George pledged returning to his conversation with the others. "As I was saying," he continued, "Henry and I were talking just yesterday that we might be able to offer some Christian kindness to the workers' families at Old Forge by setting up a school in Ironmaster Bietsel's old house after he's moved into the fine new one Henry and the masons have been finishing up."

A few of the men nodded in approval.

"A school? What a wonderful idea!" squealed a voice from just outside the circle of men.

George looked in the direction of the comment and was shocked to discover Rebecca whose outburst had just cost her the inconspicuous status she was attempting. He flashed a slight smile at her, but quickly continued his comments to the others with a stepped up enthusiasm to draw their attention away from her.

Rebecca took a step back, angry at herself for blurting out, but determined to hear what George was saying. *Why can't I control this mouth of mine,* she scolded herself. Noting that no one but George had paid her any heed, she perked up her ears again.

George continued, "If Ironmaster Bietsel approves the idea – *und er ist ein guter Mann* – we'll need benches, slate boards, an iron stove, teacher's desk and more. I think *Herr* Bietsel might even consider covering the wages for the teacher."

"The congregation could help provide the supplies," offered Joseph Frantz. "But the teacher? That's not so simple. Schoolmaster McKeon has all he can handle with Burns Hill School and, with the farms and mills and trades, we're all short of manpower in the area.

"What about a School*mistress*?" asked Rebecca clamping her hand on her mouth in frustration as soon as she had spoken.

"A woman!" Enoch Gear said incredulously. Everyone pivoted, aghast at the unexpected feminine opinion, and stared at Rebecca.

"Yes," Rebecca confirmed a little more softly, painfully aware of all the shocked expressions, but digging her heels in slightly rather than retreating.

"I'd allow *no* woman in *my* family anywhere near Old Forge," growled Enoch looking directly at Rebecca.

Rebecca cringed and withdrew from him a bit as George slid between them facing Enoch. "I agree, Brother. It could take some effort, but I'm sure we could find some sturdy, educated *fellow* to suit the cause."

George put his arm across Enoch's back and subtly guided him away from Rebecca. Enoch slowly relinquished his stare at her as she continued a tenuous escape. "In fact," George continued vigorously to Enoch, "up my way, towards Chambersburg, I know a circuit riding preacher named Thomas Ross, a formidable man with plenty of book knowledge, unmarried, who just suffered a permanent injury to his arm. He just might . . ."

As the day's activities were winding down, Rebecca stayed as close to Henry and Susan as she dared without arousing suspicion. She scanned the crowd as unobtrusively as possible. *Surely George will come to find Henry soon. They came here together, so . . .*

"Looking for someone?" asked a familiar voice from behind her.

She winced slightly. *Oh no, it's George. What do I say?* She pasted on a smile and turned. "Oh, hello, George." She flushed as she met his gaze. "I was only . . . I mean, you . . ." She drew a deep breath and softened her grin. "I mean, thank you, George, for distracting Enoch today. I didn't intend to upset anyone. I just . . ."

"No thanks necessary, *Fräulein* Rebecca. I just wish they admired your spirit as much as I do. You shouldn't have to fear speaking your mind, though I know there are those who don't agree with me," said George.

Rebecca's eyes sparkled. "But what an admirable mission you've taken on, George."

George's heart jumped at hearing Rebecca say his name again.

She clasped her hands under her chin. "To help the children of those poor folk at the forge rather than look the other way, to help them find an easier path in life is . . ."

"Rebecca!" boomed Daniel Royer, his deep voice startling them both. "Get to the wagon. Now!"

"Papa, I . . . ," she pleaded.

"*Jetzt!*" he snarled.

As she scurried past, Daniel hooked her upper arm. He scowled at her and then at George who hadn't moved. "An iron forge is no place for any woman, *certainly* not any from under *my* roof. Do the Lord's work as you like in such a place, young man," he said to George. "I'll not oppose such a cause, but no daughter of *mine* will be part of that plan,"

Then shifting his focus, he tightened his grip on Rebecca. George's stomach dropped when he saw her back stiffen and knees buckle slightly. Daniel continued, "There will be no more mention, public or otherwise, of *women* being involved. Do I make myself clear, Rebecca?" She closed her eyes and nodded.

"*Gut.*" He shoved his cowering daughter toward the wagon, punctuated his message with a sneer of warning directed at George and then followed Rebecca.

God protect her, George prayed watching them leave. Every muscle in his body contracted to control the urge to run to Rebecca and whisk her away from her father's burning anger. *I swear,* he pledged to himself, *she won't be with him for long. I won't let her endure such rage. Some day we'll be together – as man and wife – I swear. Some day soon.*

-14-

Life at Old Forge

 "Can't believe how much molasses these folks eat," said George perched atop a wooden stool as he pored over the Old Forge company store records. The long, story-and-a-half stone building that housed the store, office and some dormitories for transient workers was often pushed for storage room when new shipments arrived by wagonload on their return trips from hauling iron to the nearest point of shipment many miles away. George was responsible for the store's inventory, warehousing, ordering, payments and more with the help of the Ironmaster Bietsel's second son, John.

A loud stomping on the wooden front porch drew George's attention as Arthur Calimer, one of the company's lead teamsters, knocked clods of dirt from his boots. The heavy, cross-bucked door opened. "Afternoon," said the tall, wiry man who made his way to the waist-high counter opposite George.

"Looks like you've got the pox," laughed George looking at the splatters of dark mud that speckled the man from head to toe.

"Like to drown in the flood of gunk the mules kicked up draggin' those logs to Danny Stoops up at the new charcoalin' pit. Cleaned some of it offen my hands and face at the runnin' pump out front. Saw the notice posted 'bout the new school. I'm guessin' *you* had something to do with that." Arthur grinned.

"It's Ironmaster Bietsel who made it possible," said George putting his quill pen aside and brushing his unruly hair off his wide forehead as he drew back his broad shoulders.

"Might be, but I've seen how you look after the workers and shantytown folks along Gap Road." He pulled an odd-looking bill from a leather pouch and shoved it across the countertop. "Two plugs of longleaf tobacco," he said. "Before *you* started runnin' the store with John Bietsel, it took *two* bills of scrip to buy this much chew. And this 'company money' ain't good no place but here. Flour 'n cheese 'n the like are cheaper, too, with you tending the place. Don't think folks haven't noticed."

"Don't have to draw blood to make a profit," said George with a smile. He took two small dark brown blocks of compressed tobacco from the large crock on the shelf behind him and handed them to Arthur.

Arthur clamped his yellowed molars on the corner of one and gnawed on it while twisting it with his hand until a portion broke off. He rolled the bite around with his tongue and then tucked it in the

153

corner of his cheek. "Like I said, you care. Can't tell me it wasn't you who put the bug in the ironmaster's ear 'bout this new school."

"George, what's this school ever'one's jawin' 'bout?" asked Hattie Bumbaugh bursting in the door, an infant planted on her left hip and a toddler dangling from her right hand. "You know I can hardly read. That sign posted by the pump out front – is that about a new school comin'? Is it true, what everbody's sayin'? 'Cause if it ain't, there's gonna be hell to pay for those who told me it is."

"Now calm down, Mrs. Bumbaugh," George said holding up his hands. "They've been truthful with you. Ironmaster Bietsel's old house, now that he and his family have moved into their new one, is going to be a school for the children of company workers. Soon as the benches are in place and supplies are gathered, they'll be sending word to Thomas Ross, the new schoolmaster."

"God bless, you, George," cried Hattie. "That school will be a godsend to my young'uns. Give them a chance that . . ."

"And here's a start on those supplies," announced Henry Reighart coming around the corner with some books tucked in one elbow and a stack of slate boards in the other.

"Put those here for now," said George pointing to the counter. "I'll find storage for them later."

Hattie beamed at Henry. "And God bless you, too, sir. Can't thank you enough for helping George here."

"Save your thanks for Ironmaster Bietsel," George corrected Hattie. "He's the man really responsible."

"Well, God bless us all, then," she said spinning around pulling her child along the circle with her as he giggled.

Henry waited patiently until the store's customers had gone before claiming George's attention. "Stephen Woodridge sent me for the bosh sweep to check the slope of the air vent at the blast furnace so we can make some repairs to the stone. Said he keeps it in the office under lock and key when they're not using it so no other head forger learns his 'pious secret' – the slope numbers that yield such fine iron."

George reached into the small inside pocket at his waistband for the key. "Keep the key right here along with the store's. I'll fetch the sweep from the closet in the back. Wait here, Brother."

Henry nodded.

George returned, handed Henry the long-handled tool and laid his hand on the pile of slate boards. "Appreciate the donations," he said indicating the stack of school supplies Henry had delivered.

"I'll pass that along to Rebecca. She's the one who gathered them with orders that I get them to you. *Or* you could thank her *yourself* at Sunday Meeting. You're more than welcome to join us again – *any* Sunday will please us Reigharts, *and* Rebecca Royer according to Susan, if you come along."

"Nothing I'd like better," George admitted. "Ironmaster Bietsel's fine with my not working on Sunday, but with the furnace operating every day, it's not so easy for me to properly observe the Sabbath here. The trip home takes twice as long as the one to Waynesburg *and* the scenery at home isn't nearly as pleasing."

"Brethren are meeting at the Kneppers this week. Shall I stop by here for you Saturday afternoon?"

"That would be fine, Brother." George picked up one of the books Henry had brought and examined it. He grew serious. "Rebecca's papa won't like her helping with the school. He's a harsh taskmaster that one. Wouldn't want her in harm's way for any cause I'm part of. If there's a chance . . ."

"Daniel Royer's a hard man. That's true. Susan has shared as much with me. But, she also says he provides well for them and that her mother, a kind and caring lady, is devoted to him," Henry explained.

"But I fear his temper if Rebecca's spirit gets in his way." George ran his hand slowly across the title on the rough cover of the well-used volume, *'An Easy Guide to Speaking and Writing the*

English Language Properly and Correctly.' She probably read this; held this very book, he thought.

Rebecca lifted one end of the length of twine strung with dried apples slices from its hook on the attic rafter. She slid a goodly portion of the shriveled fruit into a reed basket. *Mama said 'enough for two pies,'* she thought considering the brimming basket. *They're always a favorite at Sunday Meeting. Never any left to bring home.* She added a few extra that rested precariously on top. "Maybe if I take enough for three, we can keep one at home for Monday." Smiling, she made her way slowly down the stairs balancing the teetering pile.

"I don't know why the Lord fastens these limas to the pods so tight," grumbled Nan as she and Cate sat on the front porch just outside the kitchen shelling the latest harvest from the garden. Discarded pods littered the wooden boards between them and each girl's apron cradled small bowls filling ever so slowly with the light green kidney shaped beans.

"At least it's a job that we can do sitting in the shade," said Cate. "Not so bad on a hot summer day."

"Nan, come in here, please!" called Catherine from the kitchen.

"Yes, Mama." Nan poured her portion of beans into Cate's bowl and smoothed the wrinkles in her skirt. "Hope Mama hasn't found a standing up job in the sun for me," she said recalling her sister's words as she headed inside.

Catherine filled the last of six pottery vases lining the work table with a final bouquet of Toad Balsam from the four-square garden. She looked at Nan. "Put one in each bedroom, the parlor and Papa's office," she instructed. "Near the windows. Maybe those annoying mosquitoes will hate the odor enough to stay outside tonight."

"Yes, Mama." Nan set her empty bowl on the table and eagerly gathered all of the vases into her outstretched arms.

"Two at a time," Catherine said, catching one as it slipped from Nan's grasp.

"Yes, Mama." Nan abandoned her first attempt and took one vase firmly in each hand and bounded off. She sped away and swerved around Rebecca as they passed in the dining room nearly toppling the dried apples.

"Watch out, Nan," Rebecca said juggling her parcel.

"Set the basket right there," Catherine instructed looking in from the kitchen and pointing to the dough tray. I'll get to those pies later. You head out to the summer kitchen and help Elizabeth and Susan with the noon meal." She eyed the overflowing basket and frowned. "That looks to me like apples for *three* pies – not *two*."

"Does it, Mama?" Rebecca answered with a grin and tilt of her head as she placed her delivery as instructed.

Catherine harrumphed, but couldn't maintain her frown. "We'll see. Now get on out there. Sun's nearly overhead."

As Rebecca disappeared out the back door, Catherine heard a crash on the porch. "Not one of my favorite bowls," she sighed, picturing the shattered remains of the dishes the girls were using. She looked out the window to confirm her suspicions and saw the scattering of lima beans among the glazed shards on the porch. Cate sat motionless on the bench with her back to the window where Nan had left her. "Cate, why are you just sittin' there? Clean up that mess," barked Catherine through the window.

Cate didn't move or answer.

"Cate Royer! Stop your daydreaming!" Catherine stomped out the door. "Bad enough you've broken the bowl, but even worse you . . ." Catching sight of Cate's motionless hands lying palms up in her lap and her sagging shoulders, Catherine stopped short with alarm. She looked quickly at Cate's face. The girl's eyes stared ahead blankly and her jaw hung loosely.

Catherine dropped to her knees ignoring the jagged debris. She grasped Cate's hands and gazed at her. "Cate," she said gently. No response. She laid her palm on her daughter's drooping cheek.

"Cate, my sweet girl, can you hear me?" Catherine pleaded, studying the expressionless face for any sign of a response.

First a slow blink, then a flutter of eyelids revealed some life as Cate's chin lifted slowly from her chest. Catherine took Cate's awakening head in her hands and brushed the pale cheeks anxiously trying to bring the color back. As Cate's puzzled look begged silently for an answer from her mother, Catherine said, "It's Mama. I'm right here, Cate. It's fine."

"What happened, Mama?" she whispered. She caught sight of the broken bowl and gasped weakly. "Your bowl!" She looked at her mother, frantic for an answer as her body slowly recovered.

Catherine moved up to the bench, her heart and mind racing, and wrapped an arm around her daughter's shoulder. "Don't worry." She rubbed Cate's arm to calm them both. "You just had a little spell, that's all. Probably from the heat." She prayed her voice was convincing despite her own fearful doubt. "You just need a cool drink and a short nap. You'll see."

"But Mama . . ."

"Hush now." Catherine laid a finger on Cate's lips. "There's a nice cross breeze in the parlor. We'll just get you to the settee and let you rest a bit."

"But Mama, I feel so weak. Like my legs won't hold me. What's wrong with me, Mama?"

"I hear fine ladies down South get fits like this from the heat all the time. The vapors, I think they call it," said Catherine prattling on. "They use smelling salts, stinking things, to wake them up. You just need to let me help you lie down until it passes. You'll be feeling right as rain before you know it. Now put your arm over my shoulder and we'll walk to the parlor together."

Nan was heading down the front stairs to retrieve her next set of vases as Catherine and Cate were making their way to the parlor. "What's happened to Cate?" she asked, struck by her sister's ashen pallor.

"Heat's gotten to her is all," Catherine explained as she lowered Cate to the sofa and then lifted her legs up and cushioned her head on the damask striped pillow as she lay down. "She'll be fine after she rests a little." Catherine stroked Cate's brow reassuringly as her eyes closed in sleep. *Bitte, lieber Gott,* she thought.

Nan stood silent witness to the scene as Catherine joined her and led her gently into the hall. "She'll be fine, Nan. But we mustn't worry anyone else about this. Best we say nothing. Cate dislikes being fussed over, especially since her accident." She stopped and turned Nan around to face her. "Understand, Nan? This is a secret we must keep to help Cate."

"Yes, Mama," pledged Nan feeling the intensity in her mother's stare. "I'll say nothing. I promise."

Catherine hugged Nan. "We all know Cate would rather make us laugh than worry." Then she held her young one's shoulders at arm's length and smiled. "Now deliver the rest of the Toad Balsam and go cool your feet in the creek 'til I call you to help with supper."

161

Tiny, ramshackle, one-story houses dotted both sides of the well worn dirt lane along Gap Road. Every 50 yards or so crude chimneys or rusty stove pipes leaking dark jagged trails of smoke poked through any variety of makeshift roofing – thin sheets of tin, roughly woven mud thatching, or crudely split lengths of wood and bark. Rough gray plaster or packed dry mud sealed the rickety walls of horizontal, rough-hewn logs or vertical layers of thin, overlapping wooden planks. Ragged muslin was the only covering for the few windows cut into the sides. Scattered benches, rain barrels, rusty tools, lines of tattered diapers or threadbare clothes and other paraphernalia surrounded each dwelling. Attached to the rear wall of most was a lean-to and small corral for a forlorn milk cow or some scrawny pigs. Chickens roamed freely, skittering in all directions and roosting in low limbs of the few nearby trees. Small vegetable plots and tiny parcels of grazing land wove a jagged patchwork pattern on the land between and behind the homes on the two-to-three-acre lots.

"I've glanced down this way before, but never traveled the road any distance," remarked Henry rocking in his saddle as he and George plodded along. "Never considered how many people live along here."

"Nearly 200 men working at the forge – furnace tenders, teamsters, loggers, colliers, laborers and such. Most of those who are married live here with their families. The Monns' place is only a quarter of a mile or so away. I appreciate you taking time to stop by before we head out," said George.

A few minutes later, George pulled back on his reins and dismounted. He jumped back as a squealing runaway pig trailed by a shirtless, barefoot boy dashed in front of him in pursuit. "Good luck, Jimmy," he called after the pair. "Hope no one greased that critter."

"Well, Mr. Smith," said a lady appearing at the open front door, her head wrapped in a bandana and sleeves rolled up to the elbows. "More likely the sweat's what makes it a slippery catch." She planted her hands on her hips and grinned. "What brings you down to shantytown?"

"This," said George handing her an envelope. "Came in with the post yesterday."

Her eyes popped as she snatched the letter and stared at it. "Is it from . . .?"

". . . Roxbury." He finished her question with a smile.

"Oh, Mr. Smith," she squealed handing the note back to him. "Is it from Christina?"

"I suspect it is," he answered. "I know you've been watching for it every day since she left to be with your ailing mother. Didn't see how I could let you wait 'til I get back on Monday to find out. Shall I open it and see?"

"Yes! Lord, yes!" She pressed closer to him as he broke the seal and unfolded the paper.

"Dear, Ma," he read. "Sorry this letter is so late coming, but cousin James just now had time to write it down for me. I . . .

". . . signed, 'Your loving daughter, Christina.'" George folded the letter and handed it to Mrs. Monn who pressed it to her cheek.

"Bless you, Mr. Smith," said the weary lady, tears of relief glistening in her eyes. She looked up at Henry waiting patiently on his horse. "That's a fine friend you have here."

"He is indeed," said Henry.

She studied Henry and then George. "Are you brothers, by chance? I mean of the same parents. Your hats make you brothers of faith, I know, but are you family as well?"

"Oh, no, Ma'am," said Henry. "Just struck up a friendship here at the forge when I started doing some brick layin'. My family lives near Waynesburg, but as you might already know, George's kin live up above Chambersburg."

"Your looks don't match – curly hair and straight – broad and lean, but I've known real brothers as different as a rooster is to a rattler. Thank you kindly for taking the time to stop by," Mrs. Monn then added. "Wish I could offer you a cold drink, but the chill'en dried up the water I fetched from the runnin' pump this mornin' by not long past noon." She picked up the rope handle of the empty bucket beside the bench. "'Spect I'll send Jimmy for more when he gets back with that pig."

"Here he comes now," Henry reported tipping his head toward the opposite side of the road where the boy had disappeared earlier. "That pig's draped over his arm like it's pretty tired out. Guess Jimmy gave it a good run."

George mounted his horse. "And Henry and I've got to be making a 'good run,' too, if we mean to make evening supper. His Mama sets a tasty table."

"And she likes nothin' more than seeing someone enjoy her efforts. George has no trouble with that." Henry laughed.

-15-

The Fabric Wears Thin

"I remember riding to this *very* farm for Sunday Meeting nearly ten years ago," Susan said to Rebecca as they sat side by side on straw nests in the wagon bed. The dust kicked up by the rumbling wooden wheels rose up in a cloud behind them. The intense July sun had quickly transformed the June mud into powdery clods that burst readily into grimy puffs. Elizabeth was intent on her reading and Cate was teaching Nan the secrets of the cat's cradle with the tangle of string they worked back and forth.

Susan checked to ensure the other sisters weren't listening. She leaned into Rebecca and whispered, "Back then we were so excited about our plan for Samuel and Sarah to meet 'by chance' at the same secluded sycamore by the creek where you're to meet George *today*. Henry told me his friend's very anxious for you to come."

Rebecca blushed and continued her tale in an attempt to evade a response. "The Leshers still owned the farm back then." She poked her elbow into Susan's ribs. "You were sweet on Edward Lesher, remember that? And now the Reigharts own the farm and you're *engaged* to Henry."

Susan shook her head in wonder. "Our scheme all those years ago worked out very well. Samuel and Sarah will have their *fifth* child in just a few months. Those ten years have passed so quickly." She smiled and nodded. "I have little doubt that sycamore tree may work some wonders again today."

"*Hör mal auf, Schwester*," Rebecca snapped. "I'm as nervous as a cat already. You're only making it worse."

"Making what worse?" asked Catherine turning around from her seat on the driver's bench beside Daniel.

Rebecca hesitated . "Uh, uh . . . the itching, Susan's poison ivy rash. Her scratching will only 'make it worse,' I was telling her," she said to her mama.

"She's right, Susan. You should try to find some Deadly Nightshade by the creek at the Reigharts today. That should help," Catherine suggested, turning her attention to the horses lathering up in the heat.

Susan and Rebecca's eyes immediately locked and their faces tightened to disguise their shocked amusement. *Deadly Nightshade! The same errand we gave Samuel ten years ago so he would find Sarah.* They caught their breath, but soon burst out in giggles.

"I'm not sure why that was so funny, but laughter's always good medicine," said Catherine.

The worship service lasted the usual three hours in spite of the stifling temperature rising along with the midday sun. The women bustled around the tables preparing food and drink and chattering about recent happenings and coming events. Some broadsheets circulated among the men prompting discussions of the dismal prospects for local farming and industry.

"Without water power and lumber, we're all in a pinch," Daniel warned the half dozen men standing near him listening intently and nodding their heads.

"There wasn't a sign of an ironworks south of Mont Alto or north of Leitersburg just ten years ago. Then in 1811 that Irishman Holker Hughes built the dams and moved in the waterwheels above Glen Furney. Now hundreds of workers, many with their entire families, are buzzing around Old Forge just a stone's throw away. They're eating up lumber like hungry swine endlessly feeding those infernal charcoaling mounds and furnaces," David added in support of his father's familiar argument.

"Can't believe how fast things are changing. What about *your* family's holdings in the ironworks up at Cove Forge?" countered Patrick Mooney.

"More lumber there with a lot fewer people. Land's too hilly and rocky for much farming. In fact, they're still *clearing* the land trying to put in more crops. Not like around here," Daniel explained.

"Gettin' tougher to find a craftsman in Waynesburg willing to do work for you in a reasonable time," complained Josiah Hess. "They're puttin' in more 'n more time up at Old Forge."

"My son Henry's one of 'em," added Amos Reighart. "Your soon-to-be son-in-law, Daniel. Your Susan's gonna be washing a lot of charcoal dust from Henry's clothes along with the sand and mortar."

The young couples whose engagements had already been presented to the congregation were free to openly keep company together after the Sunday Meeting service. They relished this time on the Sabbath that allowed to them to be together free of duties. Most of them, like Susan and Henry, would celebrate a late fall wedding after the busy harvest season waned.

"Let's sit over there," Henry suggested to Susan pointing to the spreading branches of a locust tree on a slight rise beside the board and batten barn south of his family's two-story brick farmhouse. "Good view of the slope that leads to the sycamore by the creek from that hill."

"*Gute Idee!*" Susan smiled. She picked up a swift pace in the direction he indicated beckoning him to hurry along, too.

"We'd better not be too obvious," he warned. "You're staring back at that sycamore like it's sprouted horns."

"Oh, you're right." She dropped her gaze and met Henry's teasing hazel eyes as she waited for him.

"We'll know soon enough what's happened or not happened between them. Though I think not much has been left to chance," said Henry.

"I agree," said Susan smoothing her skirt as she sat on a mossy hillock next to the old tree trunk. "But it'll be grand to know for sure."

"While we're waiting," Henry suggested, pulling a few nearby stalks of Queen Anne's Lace and presenting them to Susan, "maybe we can talk more about our own plans. We shouldn't wait much longer to secure a place to live after we've married. There're parcels of new land opened up – some for lease, others for sale – just north of the Cochran farm. I believe I could manage with what I've saved from my mason's wages to buy about five acres or so for a small house and barn." He sat down next to her.

"Really, Henry? That sounds wonderful." She hugged the bouquet of wild flowers. "Close to town, but far enough away to avoid the noise and allow us a nice sized piece of land."

"I've been talking with Papa," Henry explained. "If we buy the land, it'll be some time, a few months at least, until the house can be ready. We might need to stay with one of our families until then. I'll understand if you . . ."

"If I say 'yes?'" she said quickly. "Henry, as long as we're together, the place isn't so important."

Henry gave her a mischievous smile. "I wish *we* were hidden down by the creek right now," he said. "Because I do so want to kiss you, Susan Royer."

She blushed. "And I, you, Henry Reighart."

"Where's Cate?" asked Elizabeth eyeing the family's unpacked basket of dishes on the large table.

"Mama sent her to the wagon to fetch the apple pies," answered Nan as she placed the large tin pitcher of cooled cider she had just drawn from the keg by the front porch on the unset table. "But that was before I went to get the drink."

"With Rebecca gone to search for some Deadly Nightshade down by the creek for Susan's poison, we need all the help we can get," said Elizabeth. "It's not like Cate to shirk her duties."

"I'll go check the wagon," Nan offered.

"All right," Elizabeth agreed. "But don't be long. Mrs. Reighart will be ringing the dinner bell any time now and Papa and the brothers will soon be starting over this way. I'll go help Mama slice the bread."

Nan took off at a run around the far corner of the farmhouse where the visiting wagons had taken their place hours earlier. "Cate!" she called "Are you here?"

Hearing no response, Nan turned on her heels to search elsewhere when she noticed Maggie pawing the ground. "What is it girl?" she asked, stopping to stroke their mare's mane and investigate. When she leaned her head against the horse's silky neck, she caught sight of a pair of small, dusty boots peeking around the edge of the back wagon wheel of the family rig.

 "Cate?" she called as she made her way around to the side of the wagon. She sidestepped gingerly as her foot nearly landed in the pile of baked apples and pastry that seeped out from under an overturned pie tin on the ground. From the corner of her eye she spied the other pie still safe under the driver's bench. A distinct trail in the dust led from the upturned pan to where Cate sat in the dirt, propped against the wagon wheel with her shoulders slouched and chin lying on her chest. "Cate," Nan repeated cautiously. Cate showed no response.

Nan stepped closer and crouched down beside her sister who weakly lifted her head trying to blink her eyes open. The lids hung heavily. "Nan?" she murmured.

"Yes, Cate. It's me, Nan. Are you all right?" She took Cate's limp hands in her smaller ones.

"I . . . I don't know," answered the disoriented girl.

"Nan! Cate! What's happened?" Elizabeth's alarmed voice rang out from the front end of the wagon.

"Oh, Elizabeth," Nan replied, her voice shaking. "I suppose it's another spell – that's what Mama called it – like she had a few days ago when she was shelling the limas. Mama said it was the heat, but Cate looks much worse now than she did then."

Elizabeth laid the back of her hand on Cate's forehead and pale cheek. "No fever," she pronounced. She cupped Cate's face in her hands and searched her sister's eyes. "Cate, does your stomach ache? Are you hurting anywhere?"

Cate shook her head. "I'm just so weak. My legs folded under me before I could catch myself." Suddenly remembering the moment, Cate looked past Elizabeth to the ground. "Oh no, the pie! What'll Mama say? I didn't mean . . ." She struggled in an attempt to stand.

"Don't worry about that." Elizabeth pushed gently on Cate's shoulder to calm her. "There's still one left and the sweets table is never wanting. That other silly pie will never be missed. You just rest another minute and then Nan and I will help you get on your feet."

Nan whispered in Elizabeth's ear, "Mama said earlier that I wasn't to say anything about Cate's spell so as not to worry anyone and upset Cate even more."

"I think that's still wise advice 'til we can talk to Mama later," Elizabeth confided in Nan. "You hurry back and let them know we're coming as soon as we clean up the 'accident' with the pie. If Mama starts to question you more, try to let her know quietly what's happened. I'll come along with Cate as soon as she's able."

"*Ja, Schwester*," said Nan as she kissed Cate's bonnet. "You'll be just fine, Cate. See you soon. I love you." She scooped the remaining pie from the wagon and sped away.

George rolled the small, flat river stones he had gathered from the creek bank around in his hand to keep it from quaking. The inside rim of his hat was saturated by the heat of the day and his acute anxiety about the pending encounter. *Stay calm, now. Don't scare her off, but be clear. Love – that's what I feel, Rebecca – love.* He laid one of the stones level in the fingers of his free hand and side-armed it across a mirrored stretch of the stream undisturbed by any current. The projectile skipped numerous times across the smooth surface before disappearing in the ripples of a lazy rush where the water dropped a level.

"Wow, a four-hopper," said Rebecca who had just arrived at the secluded scene. "I'm beginning to think you must be skilled at just about everything, *Herr* Smith."

Although he'd been expecting her, the voice still startled him ending his nervous preoccupation with rehearsing what he might say to her. As he spun around, the practiced dialogue evaporated. "Rebecca!" he blurted before he could calm his tone.

"You weren't expecting me?" she asked, confused by his response.

"Of course I was," said George closing his eyes and shaking his head at his reaction. "I've thought of little else all week. You startled me because I was *still* thinking – worrying actually, about what I would say to you today. I want it to be *right*, but I've been chasing the best words for my feelings like cat after a butterfly." He dropped the stones and moved a step closer, encouraged by her smile. "Nothing I've come up with feels good enough, special enough . . ." He looked at her tenderly. ". . . for you."

"Say it simply then," she suggested, "and truly."

Drawing a deep breath, he moved to just a pace in front of her. Though he towered over her, a sweet vulnerability defined every inch of his powerful frame. His broad, calloused fingers delicately lifted her chin. "I 'simply' love you, Rebecca. 'Truly' I do."

Throwing her arms around his neck, she whispered in his ear, "I love you, too. So very much I can hardly stand it."

George wrapped her in a bear hug, picked her up and swirled in a circle until they both started laughing. Then he set her down and, after a lingering look, they kissed.

When their lips parted, they continued to hold each other, but both instinctively checked the scene around them, well aware that such actions were not proper. Assured they had not been observed, they broke into huge grins. George stole another quick kiss and then released Rebecca, but snatched back her hand and led her down to the creek.

"It means the world that you care for me," George explained, but the dimples faded from his cheeks as he grew serious. "But what am I to do about your papa?"

Rebecca's expression sobered also, knowing well George's concerns. Having no solution to offer, she merely shook her head.

"He's said nothing, but your papa's disapproval of the Old Forge School is clear," George continued. "Even more disturbing is his anger at you because you want to help. And he associates both of those with me. I can't think he'll look kindly on our being together until his dissatisfaction about the school passes, *if* it passes."

"What you say is true. Papa mildly approves women having some education, as long as we read only *The Bible* and proper books. But sadly he sees little sense in educating laborers who would be wasting time learning skills they have no use for when they should be working." She folded her hands. "You must know that I don't share Papa's feeling, but I've not spoken to him about it."

"And you mustn't," George warned her taking hold of her shoulders. "Don't ever cross him. If he questions you about your work at the school, deny it. Though that's a lie, deny it." His eyes narrowed. "If he ever raises a hand to you, come to me at once and we'll deal with whatever happens. Promise me."

Rebecca, dumbstruck by George's intensity, said nothing. George tightened his grip on her shoulders and repeated, "Promise me you'll be safe until we can be together."

"I promise," she vowed weakly. "But *you* must promise *me* to be patient. Papa will forget about the school if we're careful not to make mention of it. Then we can speak to him about us – our love. Promise me you'll wait."

George took her hands in his and kissed her tenderly. "There will never be another in my life. That I promise you. You're not yet 17, though all of a woman to me. I can wait if I know you'll be safe until the time is right. We have all the time we need. Now that I know you love me, too, I promise you we'll be together someday."

-16-

Complications Abound

Being the only physician in town, Dr. Bonebreak's office was rarely unoccupied during business hours when he wasn't called away on some emergency or making his regular circuit of house calls for those too ill or without means to travel to see him. Catherine and Cate sat together on the simple wooden bench facing the window that framed a view of West Main Street.

Young, towheaded Ben Martin bounded out of the adjoining examination room with an exaggerated fling of his left arm. His mother, Isabelle was on his heels and grabbed the waistband of his breeches. "Be careful, Benjamin! You'll be breaking that arm again before we get back to the house."

"But it feels so good to be rid of that awful splint," he countered. "I can't wait to get into a game of rounders with the fellas again."

"And your papa can't wait to have your help with the milking and harvesting, for sure." She released her hold and patted him on the head.

"Even that'll feel grand," he admitted.

"*Guten Tag, Frau* Royer – Cate," said *Frau* Martin, nodding at them, but keeping a watch on her rambunctious boy.

"*Guten Tag*," they replied.

"Looks like you have your hands full," added Catherine. "My little Nan's the only one of my children still young enough to scurry about so, and she'll soon catch up to Cate here." She indicated her daughter and Cate smiled.

As Benjamin and his mother left the office, Cate sighed. "I hope *Doktor* Bonebreak can heal my ailment as easily as he did Benjamin's arm."

Catherine patted Cate's hand. "Whatever he says, the Lord will give us strength."

"The butternut was especially good today," said Jacob wiping his last bite of bread crust across his plate to sop up the remaining drips of butter that had melted through his food.

"The garden harvest's been bountiful this summer," said Susan scraping the last spoonful of rosy rhubarb sauce from her bowl.

"More than enough cucumbers to put by a nice stock of pickles, dill and sweet," Catherine said.

"Speaking of harvest," said Daniel as the others at the noonday table finished their substantial meal, "it appears we'll have plenty of corn and wheat as well. I've determined that if I'm to be here when that work begins in earnest, then I must leave for Cove Forge tomorrow." He glanced out the window of the summer kitchen where the breezes blew more freely than in the manor's stuffy dining room. "The longer days and full moon will make safer traveling if the day's trip gets too long."

"Then I have to get a few things together to send to Samuel's family," Catherine said. "I was hoping to make the trip with you one day soon, *mein Mann*, but I think I should stay close to home right now. Samuel's Sarah should be near her time for their next child. Five grandchildren, Daniel. Hardly to be believed. Happily, her mother'll be with her for the next month or so 'til that's settled."

"I intend to make at least one more trip after this before winter sets in. Perhaps you can come along then," Daniel suggested.

"We'll see what comes," Catherine answered evasively.

"You really should, Mama," said Cate rising and stepping behind the bench to gather empty plates and bowls. "We'll manage while you're gone." The two shared a knowing look. "Really," she added softly.

"Cate speaks for all of us," said Susan. Everyone nodded in agreement as Cate headed toward the wash sink with an armload of dishes.

Catherine smiled at their encouragement. "You've all grown up right and responsible. And those little ones up north will soon . . ."

"I smell something burning," David interrupted with a sharp sniff and lift of his head as he scanned the room.

Daniel jumped from his chair staring straight ahead past the length of the table to the glowing open hearth beyond. "Cate! Get away from the fire!" All heads turned to see a stream of smoke rising close behind her where she leaned against the wall next to the large fireplace. But Cate remained frozen and staring, unfazed by the shouts that followed.

Before Catherine could rotate out of her chair or one of Cate's siblings could slide out from the long, shared benches, Daniel, already standing up, flew past them and grabbed Cate roughly by the arm. "Are you deaf, girl?" he hollered. He yanked her severely toward him and raised his hand to strike, though Cate did nothing to resist his onslaught.

Catherine turned and lunged at Daniel just in time to block his arm. "No, Daniel!" she yelled.

Daniel kept his grip on Cate, but turned his hard glare toward Catherine. "Step away, *meine Frau*. How dare you . . . ," he snarled.

"Look at her, Daniel," Catherine pleaded. He held his place. "Look at her, I beg you." She pulled Cate to her with her free arm as Daniel watched, fighting to hold his temper. "She's not well. She doesn't hear you."

Nan squeezed between Cate and Daniel to protect her sister as well while Jacob stomped on the hem of the smoldering dress. The rest looked on as a stunned Daniel stepped away and allowed

Catherine and Nan to support Cate and lead her to the nearby rope bed against the wall where they laid her down.

In the heavy silence, Daniel joined them, stupefied by Cate's appearance as she lay inert on the bed. He knelt beside her and brushed her forehead above her closed eyes. "Nan, stay here with her. Catherine, come into my office," he said flatly. He rose and moved toward the door acknowledging no one. Catherine bent to kiss Cate's cheek and followed her husband.

As the door shut behind them, the other girls flew to their sister's bedside. Jacob and David took their seats at the table, Jacob holding his head in his hands and David in a daze.

Elizabeth moved to her mother's abandoned chair. "I have to tell all of you what Mama shared with me today, about Cate." She glanced at the sleeping girl surrounded by her sisters. "Our dearest Cate."

After briefly describing the earlier fits Cate had suffered, Elizabeth went on to explain, "*Doktor* Bonebreak examined her yesterday. He said that the blow to her head at the Love Feast may have left an injury deep in her brain. 'Acquired epilepsy' is the term he told Mama and Cate. She can have small seizures like the one today anytime, without any warning. She'll blank out, lose strength and then sleep for a short time to recover."

"When will she get better?" asked Susan.

"There's no medicine, no cure. She may go for quite awhile with no seizures, but they usually recur eventually." Elizabeth's voice cracked. "For the rest . . . the rest of her life."

Daniel stared at his hands folded atop his desk as Catherine studied her swollen knuckles. They were unable to face each other until they processed the truth of their daughter's condition and harnessed their emotions. After a prolonged silence, Daniel sat back and rested his arms across his chest. He coughed to steady his voice and looked at his wife. "You ought not to have kept this from me. We've got to decide together what's to be done."

She gave her husband a fleeting glance and nodded as she looked up and away to fend off impending tears. Daniel continued in a strained, businesslike way. "You know far better than I do how to run a household. The first consideration must be the safety of everyone who lives here. We should consider the possible risks." He stood, moved behind her and placed his hands on her shoulders. "The week I'm away will give you time to solve this dilemma. Pray God you're wiser than me in this, because I see very few happy choices."

Catherine wrung her hands. "But Daniel, we can't . . ."

"Let's say no more until I've returned. Nothing in haste. Nothing before much prayer and thought." He kissed the top of her head and left her in stunned silence.

Jacob pulled aside the curtain at his bedroom window. The aura of the mottled full moon pulsed in the night sky and washed the arching maples along the front lane and the rolling hills beyond with an eerie sheen. *Why Cate? How can Mama bear this? How will we . . .?*

"Has *Vater* spoken to you about the drop in milling profits?" David asked as he pored over the notes in front of him on the small desk at the other side of the bedroom they shared.

"What?" Jacob turned to his brother aghast at the mention of such a topic at this emotional time.

"The profits at the mill," he repeated with impatience, unaware of Jacob's disdain. "With so many other mills close by, you might . . ."

"Another time, David," Jacob scolded. "Our sister is . . ."

"Our sister is sick, I know. It's sad, very sad," barked David. "But life still goes on and someone needs to see to the necessities that keep the family's place in it. With the tannery, the farm, the mill, the ironworks up north – too much work, not enough workers, more and more competition, just to mention a few things – *Vater* is stretched to the limit without any added burdens." He rose and met Jacob nose to nose. "I'm the eldest son, the next in line. My *first* duty after service to God is service to our *Vater*. I can't afford the luxury of sadness. You chastise me for not feeling, but my role is to support *Vater*."

"What you can't afford," Jacob growled in a rare display of anger, "is to hurt Mama and our sisters. How can you speak of Cate as a 'burden' when she's brought so much joy to all of us?"

"The truth is hard. Cate is a sweet, loving soul, but her condition does present obvious problems. Our sisters, especially Elizabeth, being the oldest unmarried daughter, will be Mama's support in this. We'll all do as we can for the good of the family. Now I suggest *you* consider how the mill can turn a better profit." He stared hard at Jacob.

Jacob pushed him briskly aside and moved to the door. He flung it open and turned his head glaring at David. "And I suggest that *you* soften your heart before your soul turns to stone. *Vater* gives our family more than its full measure of hard practicality for now." He stormed out slamming the door behind him.

An early dusk beckoned the entire Royer family to the cool, still air of the spreading elm by the creek. The first scattered notes of the impending cricket chorus sounded faintly as light pink clouds streamed across the darkening sky. "I love the crickets' tune, but they'll soon wake up the mosquitoes that'll chase us back inside," said Nan, stringing yellow dandelion blooms into a chain.

Even David had pulled himself away from his work desk and stood at the edge of the family gathering facing the north horizon. "I suspect *Vater* will be home in a day or two. It's been nearly a week since he left."

"Should be so," said Catherine slowly rocking the slat back swing hanging from a low, sturdy branch. "No doubt he'll miss the cooler mountains of Huntingdon County when he returns."

"Well, while we're here together," announced Cate moving from her seat on the grass next to Rebecca and Susan to her mother's side on the swing, "I'd like to say something." She took in all the faces that had turned to her request. "To all of you."

She waited as the girls took seats on the ground closer to the swing. Jacob and David moved in a bit caught up in the family's somber anticipation as Cate began. "Since Papa left, we've all been silent about my illness, but I believe it's been heavy in all of our hearts." Catherine took Cate's hand and lowered her head. "This morning, I finally stopped asking God 'why' because, you see, that doesn't really matter. 'Why' was getting in the way of discovering the good that can be gotten from my affliction." Catherine looked up a little stunned.

"For one thing, I've never enjoyed solitude," Cate continued "Being alone is no comfort for me, and especially now, if we're all to be safe, I'll not be left alone again. Someone I love will almost always be with me. How can that be bad?

"Besides, I'm still able to do many things – see, smell, hear, walk, talk, work, think, pray and more. But most of all, I can still laugh and love. Each of us needs to feel we contribute, have a purpose. I've decided that my most important task is to make sure that my companions, whoever they are, share smiles with me." She stretched her neck looking past the girls in front of her and spied her brothers. "Even you, David – and Papa!" Everyone, including David, couldn't help but smile.

"See!" she pointed at David. "I've already started my job." She leapt to the ground and hugged Susan, Rebecca and Nan. Elizabeth moved behind the swing and wrapped her arms around Catherine's neck as Jacob and David stared at Cate in admiration. Everyone's eyes but David's glistened, but even he had a catch in his throat that he had to lightly cough away.

-17-

Cove Forge

"We should be making the move in the next few days, Papa. We'll be settled just in time for Sarah's *Mutter* to come and the newest baby to arrive." Samuel dismounted his chestnut horse and strode toward the small front porch of the two-story limestone house. "Sarah hopes this child has my fair hair since the first four are brown-headed, like the Provines."

"All of them are fine looking, hardy children," Daniel commented "The Lord has blessed you. And now a new home – you've done well, Samuel."

"*Danke*, Papa. The business is thriving. The first 80 acres you and your brother bought in 1811 made the Cove Forge furnace possible. Thanks to the 3,000 acres of timber, ore, and limestone at The Barrens and the acres at Springfield Farm and Forge we've added since then, we're one of the most productive furnaces in the region. As ironmaster, I'll be much closer to the Springfield operations now that the Youngs have sold us this house and parcel of land."

Daniel laid both hands on the pommel of his saddle and surveyed the structure from his elevated perch. "Fine home, indeed. And I can see why you've added the east rear wing. You're going to need the extra space for your growing family." He lowered himself to the ground and walked to the west side of the building for a better view of the new construction. *Samuel's a good man. He brings out the best in people, always has. And Sarah's his equal in many ways,* he thought.

Daniel glanced down a slight grade some 50 feet away to a swiftly running stream and small, stone, sloped-roof structure. "The Youngs built an impressive spring house as well."

"Can't say I'm as impressed with the mason's work on the main house," said Samuel pointing out the walls' limestone surface. "Stones are too rough and unfinished." Then he opened the heavy six-panel front door flanked by sidelights and examined the wood frame. "No lintels on any of the doors and windows either. The new work should be much finer, more like the masonry on our house in Waynesburg." Then he buffed the intricate iron railing shaped in delicate grapevines that supported the porch roof, unlike the wooden beams of the Royer mansion in Waynesburg. "But I *do* admire this fine ironwork. Doesn't leave much doubt as to my profession."

Daniel craned his neck toward Samuel for a distant inspection of the railing and nodded. Then he continued his survey of the recent wing stretching out behind the house and smiled. "The two-story porch definitely reminds me of our addition at home."

Samuel came around the corner to join his father. "I couldn't help but notice the resemblance of this house to our family place as soon as I saw it. When I designed this wing, maybe I was trying to bring a part of Waynesburg up north."

Daniel stepped up onto the large sideporch and examined one of the wooden posts. "Hard to believe it's been almost nine years since you came here to work at the ironworks with your uncle." He sat on a rough hewn bench by the side door. "Do you miss home?"

Samuel sat beside him. "Sarah and I both miss the families we left behind, but we've come to love these mountains, even if they're pretty remote compared to Waynesburg. All but our oldest were born here and they're thriving. Not many of our kindred Brethren around, but enough to keep up customs. Not as many folks in general here, but more variety. Scotch-Irish have the majority along with Welsh mine workers and the like. We all blend well and help each other whenever there's a need, regardless of our beliefs or background."

Daniel nodded.

"It's been good for John, Papa. *Sehr gut*. He's been an excellent worker and support for Sarah and me." Samuel paused to let Daniel consider this delicate subject. The eight-year alienation between his father and younger brother caused by their differing views on the War of 1812 had not been resolved. John's eagerness to fight the British had run afoul of the Brethren's pacifist beliefs. With the war over, Samuel hoped his father and brother might reconcile despite their stubbornness and pride.

Daniel continued to stare ahead. "Many hurtful things were said before John left home. It was a terrible time. I'm sure he's shared as much with you." He leaned forward, elbows on his knees, and propped his chin on his clasped hands. "Since then I've lost a daughter and newborn grandson, and now Cate's affliction is with us. Those losses can't be helped." He looked back at Samuel. "Perhaps we should save those that we can."

"John would welcome the chance, Papa." Samuel laid a hand on Daniel's back. "The family would be overjoyed to see him at Susan's wedding to Henry Reighart. I could certainly spare him from work for such a special occasion."

Daniel only nodded.

Samuel stood. "Now let me show you the rest of the house, so we can make it back to Cove Forge before dark."

"We'll tie up our wagon behind the Sweet Shoppe," Jacob told Elizabeth who held the reins in the smaller of the two enclosed black buggies in front of the family barn. "There should be room for yours too, if we both get to town soon enough."

"It's always a challenge on Market Days, but we'll follow you and hope," Elizabeth agreed.

Jacob nodded and went to join Catherine, Cate and Nan in the other buggy. He hopped up beside his mother. "Everyone ready?"

"Like bears for honey," said Cate. "Right, Nan?"

"Grrrrrrr." Nan growled curling her hands like claws.

They all chuckled as Jacob snapped Maggie's reins.

A premature fall breeze sharpened the air and heightened the intensity of the lightly tinged leaves against the blue sky. Elizabeth shook the reins to urge Elsie to keep up the pace. "It's a perfect day for a picnic." She tilted her head toward Susan and Rebecca jiggling around in the back.

 Rebecca steadied the carefully packed basket and smiled at Susan. "And with Papa in Cove Forge and David at home, George and I needn't worry about being seen. I'm so glad you and Henry invited us along with you."

"I'm happy they could both take time from work," said Susan. "They were going to finish some jobs this morning, but said to meet them just after noon at the meadow below Snowberger Hill."

"*Ach*, I can hardly wait," said Rebecca wrapping her arms around herself.

"You two are as excited as dogs at a butcherin'" Elizabeth laughed shaking her head.

"That may be," said Susan, "but I love the feeling. *Es ist wunderbar.*" She poked her head up beside Elizabeth's. "Libby, haven't you ever, *ever* seen a man who made you catch your breath, made your heart beat a little faster, or at least made you smile for no reason?"

Elizabeth's expression froze as she hesitated.

Susan looked back wide-eyed at Rebecca, shocked that Elizabeth hadn't answered immediately – that their eldest sister might surprise them both with a confession that she had actually noticed a man.

Elizabeth fumbled with the reins, but remained silent.

"Who?" squealed Susan.

"Who is it?" Rebecca repeated excitedly squeezing in between the two.

"You must tell no one," commanded Elizabeth. "I probably shouldn't say anything. It's probably nothing. He hasn't really . . ." She wriggled in her seat.

"Who?" they nearly shouted in unison making Elizabeth wince.

"His name is David Good," she said almost in a whisper. "His family runs a mill south of our farm. We met when I was at Snow Hill a few months ago. He was blacksmithing for them."

"What happened? What did he say?" Rebecca quizzed her.

"Nothing really," she sputtered. "But the way he looked at me, I felt . . . special."

Susan clapped her hands and Rebecca giggled.

Elizabeth finally relaxed and smiled. "And he took great pains to be where I was as often as he could." She sighed. "He said that he hoped I would miss him."

"Did you kiss him?" Rebecca asked.

Elizabeth turned her head away, but nodded. Susan hugged her. "*Ist sehr gut*," she said.

"*Sehr, sehr gut*," Rebecca echoed.

Tufts of rye grass sprung up around the edges of the heavy woolen blanket spread just below the split-rail fence that marked the border of the Snowberger acres. Susan wrapped the remains of the crumbly peach shortcake in a cloth and fastened it with a piece of string. "Has everyone had their fill?" she asked tucking the bundle into the basket next to the dishes and other leftovers from the picnic.

Henry lay on the ground with his head to the top of the slightly sloped grade. His hands cushioned the shock of straight hair at the nape of his neck and his hat was tilted forward shielding his eyes from the mid-afternoon sun. "I've had my fill of food, but I can't get enough of this day and this company."

"Must say I agree," said George as he pulled a small handful of grass and held it a few feet from the ground releasing it slowly to let the breeze carry it across Rebecca's face as she examined a small book of verse he had brought along to share with her.

Rebecca sputtered as the chaff caught her nose. She put the volume aside and retaliated with a fistful of grass aimed directly at George's dimples as they both laughed.

"Your sister Cate sounds very wise for a 14-year-old," said Henry sitting up to take a draught of spring water from his leather-bound canteen. He readjusted his hat, swallowed and sighed. "So unfair that the innocent suffer. And it's a weight your whole family bears." He looked at Susan and Rebecca. "I know how much you both care for her."

Susan sat next to Henry, pulling up her knees and smoothing her skirt modestly to her ankles. "You're right, Henry. She's very precious, always finding the joy of a situation. She simply refuses to be sad."

"And I 'refuse' to leave here 'til we absolutely have to," said Rebecca retrieving her book and hugging it. "I almost hate to give this back to the school, but it'll serve so many more there." She beamed at George. "You've done a fine thing, George."

"With a lot of help and prayers." He ran his finger lightly across the top of Rebecca's arm. "Many of my prayers have been answered. Now, if only your papa could get past his objection to the school and my part in it. I'm anxious for him to look more kindly on *me*, so he could look more kindly on the idea of *us*."

Rebecca handed him the book. "In good time," she murmured.

"Only about two months 'til *our* vows," Henry reminded Susan lifting one of the ties dangling from her cap. "With luck, we'll dig the footers and root cellar on our lot next week." She smiled at him.

"Still enough time to change your mind, Susan," said George with a twinkle in his eye and an elbow poke to Rebecca.

"Still enough time to run, Rebecca." Henry laughed.

"Only if it's in the direction I'm already headed," she said.

"Before I begin tonight's devotions, I have some news to share." Daniel rested his hands on the unopened Bible on his lap and looked at the family in their accustomed seats in the parlor for the evening ritual. "First, I stopped at Snow Hill on my way home from Cove Forge today to check on the progress of their dairy herd. Happily, they're well recovered and ready to return two of the cows and the firstborn calf as agreed. Elizabeth, you and Jacob will fetch them tomorrow and I'll help Uriah Baer with the mill duties here."

"Yes, Papa," Elizabeth and Jacob answered.

Susan and Rebecca shared a knowing look that Elizabeth deliberately avoided. They were both thinking the same thing – *David Good.*

"Good." Daniel pronounced. Susan and Rebecca burst into giggles prompting a sullen stare from Elizabeth. The rest of the family was as perplexed as Daniel at this response, but his stern 'Ahem' silenced them as he continued. "Now, Cate, I'll need your help with my next item. Come over here beside me."

Cate looked as puzzled as the others, but she quickly obeyed.

Maintaining his serious demeanor, Daniel faced his daughter. "I understand from Mama that you've taken on an important responsibility while I was away and I heartily approve." Cate's face softened and the rest of the family relaxed a bit. "Now I feel I should give you some help with your task." He motioned with a wave of his hand for her to come closer. He cupped his hand around his mouth and leaned to her ear to whisper.

Within seconds, Cate grinned broadly and her eyes sparked as she listened to Daniel's secret message. She gasped and pulled away to study his face. "Really, Papa? Truly?"

"Really and truly. Now I think you should tell the rest of the family and satisfy their curiosity." Daniel leaned back in his chair to give Cate center stage.

Cate pulled herself up straight and firmly planted herself for the announcement. "John's coming to Susan's wedding! He's accepted Papa's invitation. John's coming home!"

Everyone stared at her in stunned disbelief until she nodded vigorously. "That's what Papa just told me." When Daniel's smile confirmed the unthinkable, joy immediately erased their shock. They all leapt from their seats, hugged each other with unbridled enthusiasm and praised the news as they shared loving, respectful glances with their father.

"What wonderful news, Daniel," said Catherine gazing tenderly at her husband. She closed her eyes basking in the happiness around her. *"Danke, mein Gott,"* she whispered. *"Denn mein Sohn war verloren . . .* and now he is found."

The family lingered in the softly lit parlor longer than usual warmed by the sense of a newfound harmony. The ticking of the tall Jacob Wolff clock echoed in the hall as each one read or mended or busied themselves with mindless tasks and their own thoughts. Daniel was the first to rise. "The long trip has tired me out and this old man has to fill young Jacob's shoes at the mill tomorrow, so I'm off to bed."

Catherine put aside her darning ball and needle, pushed herself from the rocking chair and took his arm. "I'll retire, too. These old bones are weary, but happy tonight."

Within a very short time, everyone had settled in to their respective rooms for the night.

"I'm still smiling so hard I can't sleep," said Cate, her head propped on the pillow as she stared out the window at the stars. The girls had spent hours whispering after they had gone upstairs to bed.

Susan and Rebecca lay next to each other in the larger bed in similar stages of calm euphoria. "Hard to remember two more wonderful days. I hate to close my eyes and let them go," said Susan.

Rebecca sighed. "Our picnic, my George, your wedding and now John and Papa reconciled." She rolled over to face Susan. "Elizabeth's news was such a surprise, but not nearly as much as Papa's."

Cate sat up and turned to them. "What was Elizabeth's news?"

Susan frowned a silent reproof at Rebecca. "Oops, sorry," Rebecca apologized. "It just slipped out."

Cate hopped on the bed beside them. "What is it? I won't tell a soul, I promise."

Rebecca looked to Susan for a reluctant nod of approval before she spoke. "A certain young man has caught Elizabeth's eye." Cate's mouth fell open, much as it had at Daniel's words earlier that evening. "She confessed to us on the way to Market Day yesterday."

"Who? When? Does anyone . . . ?" blurted Cate.

"Slow down," said Rebecca. "I'll tell you all we know, which isn't much, and then we must all try to get some sleep."

"Hard as I try, I can't remember John," said Nan as Elizabeth settled under the blanket in their shared bed in their room across the hall. "I can't wait to see him."

"You were barely a year old when he left," Elizabeth explained blowing out the candle on the nightstand. "But I'm sure he remembers you. He and Jacob were inseparable, like two peas in a pod, though they didn't look much alike. John's taller and leaner than Jacob, with lighter finer hair, more like Susan's. There'll be two causes for celebration on her wedding day, a new family begun and an old one mended." She tucked the light blanket around Nan's chin. "Now sleep. The sun will soon chase the moon away for a new day."

David trimmed the wick on the lamp on his bedroom desk, but remained seated in the darkness facing the wall as he considered his next move. Jacob had come into their room ten minutes after him, sat on the edge of the bed and said nothing. His brother's heavy silence mystified David in light of the mood earlier that evening. He finally turned to see Jacob holding his head in his hands. *What's he thinking? What's wrong?*

Respecting his brother's disquiet, David remained in his chair. "Happy news tonight," he said. "You above all, besides Mama, must have missed John the most. You and he were always together – never one without the other in your younger years."

Jacob lowered his hands and nodded, but then twisted his head away as his face contorted and tears rolled down his cheeks. David moved toward him, but Jacob held up his hand to keep him at a distance.

David stopped, but didn't retreat, at the ready if Jacob needed him.

Jacob drew a deep breath for control and said to the air, "I know you and Papa don't abide such weakness, especially from another man. But . . ." His voice cracked.

"I don't judge you on that," David said. "You've shown yourself a strong man many times over. But, I don't understand. Why? After what I thought must be such good news, especially for you, *why* are you so upset? Don't you want John to come back?"

Jacob drew his shoulders back and looked at David. "I've wanted nothing more since the day he left us. Not a day has passed since then that I haven't thought about him, turned to tell him something and found him gone, imagined his belly laugh when I heard a good joke."

"Then why are you so troubled? It's finally resolved."

Jacob brushed his tears away brusquely. "In all the time he's been gone, I've never allowed myself to feel the loss. I've pushed it away, buried it deep rather than face it every day. Now that he's coming back, I can't describe how wonderful it'll be to see him again.

But I can't stop the tears for all of the days that have been lost to us forever. It's those days I'm mourning so I can put them behind me – not let them take anything away from the good times ahead." He stared at David. "Do you understand?"

"I do, Jacob," said David slowly. "In fact, in a way I envy you such feelings. Not the pain, of course, but the equally strong affection that is its partner. I've yet to find that in my life."

Jacob studied the sincerity on David's face, the rare vulnerability he had shared. He walked to him and embraced him. "Thank you, David." David returned the embrace. "We never know what each new day might bring. We can only pray for peace for those we love."

"Thank you, too, Jacob. Tomorrow is, indeed, a new day."

-18-

Piecing the Family Quilt

The grumble of the huge millstones echoed along the heavy oak beams of the Royer mill as they pulverized the hard rye seeds into fine, tan flour. Perched high on the third floor, Uriah Baer dragged a ponderous sack of seeds from the stack Lester Cochran had delivered earlier in the week to the chute that fed the hungry maw of the machine. "Ready for more, *Herr* Royer," Uriah hollered to Daniel, laboring three stories below to capture the milled flour at the output chute.

Daniel raised his arm high and shook his head. "Just give me a minute to catch my breath," he responded as loudly as he could muster over his puffing.

"Yes, sir," said Uriah dropping his burden and taking a seat on top of it.

"Been too long since I tackled some *real* work. The years are beginning to show and they'll catch up faster if I don't keep on the move," said Daniel.

"Jacob and I stop now and then, too, *Herr* Royer. These sacks aren't easy to handle and the ones at your end weigh a lot more than the ones up here. Don't be too hard on yourself," Uriah consoled.

"Maybe I should work from your end tomorrow," Daniel suggested. "Since the sun's setting earlier and they'll have a new calf in tow, Jacob and Elizabeth will need to stay at Snow Hill tonight. So you and I will have another work day together."

"Whatever you say, *Herr* Royer," said Uriah looking at the imposing stockpile of unprocessed grain. "Harvest time is hurtin' time for *everybody's* muscles.

Elizabeth lifted her face to the mid-morning sunlight as she and Jacob urged their horses toward the outskirts of Waynesburg en route to Snow Hill. "Aah, that feels so good," she said. "Not at all like the wind and rain on the day Thomas Fahnestock, David Good and I delivered the cows nearly a year ago."

"These Indian summer days are my favorite," said Jacob taking in the kaleidoscope of fall colors tousled by a clean, brisk breeze in the treetops against a crystalline sky. "Everything's so rich and full of life."

"But the days are too short," Elizabeth lamented. "The sun goes down too soon and reminds us that winter's coming."

Jacob studied his sister silently. *She's a quiet beauty, more delicate than the others. Serious and steady.* Suddenly it struck him. *Guess I've never really thought about how she feels. Is she happy with her lot as eldest daughter – taking care of Mama and Papa - no husband or family of her own?*

Feeling his stare, Elizabeth turned her face to him. "What?" she asked.

Jacob smiled. "Just glad Papa agreed to let you come along and visit your friend. And I was wondering, since you enjoyed your time so much at Snow Hill, have you ever thought about that kind of life for yourself – like the sisters there, devoted to God and helping others? Or is staying with Mama and Papa what you want? Or do you, maybe, hope for a husband and family someday?"

Elizabeth looked away obviously troubled by the question.

Jacob sensed her unease. "Don't mean to pry, but a few days ago David told me his first responsibility as the eldest son is to support Papa. As the oldest daughter, do you feel the same about your responsibility to Mama – or to God?"

She sighed. "I thought I did, or maybe it's better to say, I 'accepted' that role in life. But . . ." She looked at Jacob with a pained expression. "I'm not at peace with that anymore. I've come to covet Melonia's relationship with God and the Snow Hill Order – to envy my sisters their prospective husbands and homes of their own – to wonder what more my life could be."

205

Jacob nodded. "I struggled for some time after Mollie left with where my life would go. My hopes were slow to fade, but each day I'm more content to be a good worker and peacemaker at home. With Samuel and John gone, and David so focused on Papa, I've left the complications of romance behind me for now. Best to concentrate on running the mill and helping keep peace between my parents and sisters."

"You've calmed the waters for us many times, Jacob. In your own quiet way, you've been our rock when the seas get rough at home," she assured him. "So strong at such a young age. You're not yet 22 – lots of years ahead of you. Plenty of time to consider other paths you might take. But I'm soon 29. Too late, I'm afraid, to find a different way. Mama had five children by the time she was my age."

"But she was 43 when Nan was born," Jacob reminded her.

"And dear Polly was only your age when she died trying to have a child. And the poor baby was lost, too," said Elizabeth shaking her head. "Do I want that kind of sadness in my life?"

"I suppose when the time comes for a change, the Lord will let us know what we should do," said Jacob.

"This'll keep the cider press busy," said Susan as she and Nan pulled the hand cart laden with four baskets heaping with ripe Baldwin apples toward the barn.

Rebecca and Cate made up a similar pair following far enough behind to avoid the dust kicked up by the rumbling wooden wheels of the first cart.

"Hope Papa uses most of these for cider and vinegar," said Cate. "The Winesaps already in the icehouse are so much tastier in pies and apple butter than these tart ones."

"I think Mama's already set the sweetest ones aside for this year's apple snitzen," Rebecca assured her. "Is the gathering at the Cochrans'" She waited for Cate's response, but oddly, none followed. Instead, Rebecca noticed Cate's side of the cart starting to lag behind. *Oh, no!* She panicked remembering Cate's condition and quickly turned to her little sister. Cate's eyes were glazed and her back foot dragged through the dust as she started to stumble.

"Cate!" Rebecca stopped instantly and released the cart just in time to catch her sister and settle her easily to the ground. "Susan! Nan! Come help," she yelled ahead as she sat down behind Cate to support her sagging body.

The two ran back and pushed the abandoned cart aside. Susan knelt and stroked Cate's pale forehead. "Mama says the spells only last a short time, but then she needs to sleep to get her strength back. Rebecca, you just stay here with her in the shade of the oak tree 'til she wakes up. Nan and I'll get the carts to the barn and then help you take her to the house."

"Good idea, Susan. Cate wouldn't want us to make a big fuss about it. You two go on. We'll be just fine here 'til you get back,

207

won't we Cate?" Rebecca said tenderly hugging her unconscious sister.

"You girls did exactly as you should," said Catherine coming over to the rows of brimming baskets lined up by the barn. "Cate's resting in the parlor. It's quiet there this time of day, so she can have some peace to recover." She looked at the quantity of fruit behind them. "Meantime, Nan, you can sort through the newest crop of apples. Separate the bruised and damaged ones for the first pressings. Susan and Rebecca, you can come help get a start on noon meal. With Elizabeth gone to Snow Hill, I can use the extra hands."

"Can we check my celery crop first, Mama? We haven't had any rain for a while. Probably needs watering," said Susan.

"Well, we can't have wilted celery at the wedding next month, now can we?" Catherine smiled. "Suppose I can spare you for awhile, but don't take too long."

"Good thing we bundled the stalks last week," said Susan as she dipped some stream water from the bucket and poured it into the shallow trenches between the ten-foot rows of light green celery. "Look how much they've grown since then. They'd have fallen over for sure if we hadn't tied them up when we did."

"This crop will be perfect by November for the wedding," said Rebecca.

"And the last harvest before frost," said Susan smiling at her sister. "We'll leave healthy crowns in the ground and cover them with mulch. Then they'll grow those sweet white flowers early next spring to make seeds for *your* wedding table celery."

"I'm more hopeful every day. Papa's been different lately. With his inviting John to your wedding and being more patient with Cate, his feelings about George might soften sooner than we thought," said Rebecca.

"He still might want you to wait 'til you're at least 18, like me. Keep you an extra year to be a help to Mama," Susan advised.

"That waiting wouldn't be so hard, as long as we knew Papa approved." Rebecca emptied her watering gourd into the row adjacent to Susan.

"I can't wait to get a look at the hearth and chimney at the new cabin," said Susan. "Henry said he's nearly finished with it. I've missed his visits in the evenings, but that's the only time he's been free to work on our place." She hugged herself. "Our place," she repeated. "Doesn't that sounds simply wonderful – 'our place?'"

"Can't imagine anything better." Rebecca ran her hand across the feathery tops of the celery stalks thinking, *Someday for George and me, too – someday.*

Elizabeth and Jacob rode the final mile to Snow Hill in silence. As they approached the familiar sight, Elizabeth thought of Melonia. A special liniment, scented with lavender from the garden, was packed away in a leather satchel tied to her saddle. *Mama said it worked well for Opa Stoner. Lord willing, for Melonia too. The candied roots I brought will surely tame that cough of hers.*

Melonia's frail appearance had haunted Elizabeth since the Love Feast. *She aged so quickly in the little time I was away. I wanted to talk to her, but then . . . Cate got hurt. There wasn't time,* Elizabeth sighed. *Hope she'll be well enough to show me how to make the ink with crushed walnut shells that Sister Zenobia uses for her calligraphy.*

As she imagined how Melonia's smile lines would crinkle when they met, David Good's face appeared unprompted in her mind. *David — what's he done since we parted? Has he given any thought to me? Maybe we'll be able to speak privately?* She shook her head to chase away such thoughts. *Stop it, Elizabeth Royer. He's probably not thought of you once this whole time. And what on earth would we talk about anyway? His place is at Snow Hill, and mine,* she thought sadly recalling her earlier conversation with Jacob, *will probably be at home.*

Sister Zenobia opened the door, took one look at Elizabeth and turned white as the kerchief pinned around her shoulders. "Oh Elizabeth, we weren't expecting you this soon."

"Oh, Sister, sorry about the disruption but Papa . . ." A dark foreboding quickly overtook Elizabeth. Something in Zenobia's sad blue eyes carried unspoken news that Elizabeth's heart didn't want to know. She looked past Zenobia toward the empty rocker by the fire. "Where's Melonia?"

"Let me take your cloak, Elizabeth. Pastor Lehman will be here soon," said Zenobia avoiding the question.

"I don't want to see Pastor Lehman," said Elizabeth, surprised by the strength in her voice. "I came to see Melonia."

"Oh, my dear child," said Zenobia, clutching Elizabeth's cloak. "She's gone to the Lord."

When a second cup of catnip tea had calmed Elizabeth enough to stop her weeping, Sister Zenobia took her hand. "Come with me." Elizabeth followed obediently, not fully comprehending that Melonia was no longer there. They climbed the stairway to the sisters' sitting room where a very large wooden cradle made of seasoned walnut stood close to the 10-plate stove.

Sister Zenobia gently rocked the adult cradle. "She spent her last days here Elizabeth. She wanted to be near us and we took turns rocking her. None of our other remedies worked, but the back-and-forth of the cradle gave her some comfort." The rocker creaked in the quiet room. "Sister Melonia never complained," said Zenobia. "She even said our chatter eased the pain."

Elizabeth caressed the smooth sides of the cradle where her friend had spent her last days.

"She was always cheerful, always trying to lift *our* spirits, right to the last. In the hours before she drew her final breath, she told us not to fear for her because by nightfall, she'd be singing with the angels and . . ." Sister Zenobia buried her face into her apron.

"Why didn't you send for me?" asked Elizabeth fighting her anger.

"Sister Hannah begged her to let us fetch you, but Melonia insisted your family needed you. She didn't want to call you away from your responsibilities there."

"But I'd have come in a moment," said Elizabeth, rocking the empty cradle as suppressed tears trickled down the back of her throat. "I would've dropped *everything*."

"Yes, Elizabeth, we knew that. And Sister Melonia did too. She said she'd see you in Heaven and that we must all look to that happy day."

The Royers of Renfrew

After a restless night in her old room in the cloister, Elizabeth joined the brothers and sisters and Jacob in a joyless breakfast. Sister Zenobia had told Jacob of Melonia's death and his sympathetic glances from across the room nearly rekindled Elizabeth's tears. When she finally emerged from the cloister building after prolonged and tearful farewells, she winced as the bright sunlight almost blinded her.

"I'll go to the barn and fetch Lulu's calf for Papa," Jacob said. "The sisters have already packed up the crocks of butter. Papa'll be happy that the first payment's made. Wait here, I won't be long."

"That's all right Jacob. I've one last thing to do. I'll meet you down by the road," she said with a resolution he'd not often heard in her voice.

Elizabeth made her way past the blacksmith's shop toward "God's Acre," the small Snow Hill cemetery just north of the creek. She passed by the somber yews and evergreens, the signs of eternal life that marked the entrance to the cemetery. Only the children's graves were covered with flowers, the last of the frost-singed petals of pink and purple phlox sheltered the tiny mounds.

 "What a peaceful spot you've chosen," she said, standing before the newly carved headstone. "How like you Melonia, to put others ahead of yourself. How I wish I could've been with you at the end, if only to say . . . to say . . ."

". . . goodbye?"

Elizabeth immediately recognized the voice behind her. *David.* She turned and saw that David Good had followed her from the blacksmith's shop to the cemetery. He looked kindly at Elizabeth and took a step toward her. "How like Melonia to bring us together once again," he said.

"Oh, David, why didn't she let me come? At least I said goodbye to Polly before she died and wished Mollie well when she left. I can't bear all these farewells. It's so hard to be the one left behind."

David stepped forward putting his arm around her shoulder. "I told the sisters that I'd ride straightaway to get you, but they said Melonia wouldn't allow it. She was a strong woman, much like you."

Elizabeth searched his eyes as David continued. "She said she wanted you to live your life as freely as she had lived hers."

Despite his comforting words, Elizabeth's frustration continued to gnaw at her. "And just what do you think *that* means?" she asked almost spitting the words. "Such vague advice. I need her wisdom, not some empty phrase."

David waited silently until Elizabeth's fists unclenched and her jaw relaxed. Then he pointed to the inscription on the tombstone. "Maybe there's some meaning in this."

> *And soft be thy repose,*
>
> *Thy toils are o'er, thy troubles cease,*
>
> *From earthly cares in sweet release*
>
> *Thine eyelids gently close.*

"Maybe you'll have to find the peace you seek on your own."

"But how can I find peace in this torment?" said Elizabeth her voice trembling. "My soul craves the life of the cloister, but duty dictates I stay at home."

"I know, Elizabeth," said David lifting her chin to meet his gaze. "But what does your heart say?"

Elizabeth found the answer in his kiss.

"Nine years," John said softly as he reined his horse to a halt at the end of the lane leading to the Royer manor house. He hung his hat on his pommel and wiped the sweat from his high forehead with the back of his gloved hand. Replacing the hat, he thought with a measure of disbelief, *I was only 14 when I left with the*

few gold coins from Mama strung 'round my neck. He pushed his heels down feeling the metal stirrups through his boots firmly pressing against the balls of his feet. *I could barely stay in the saddle back then.*

John swung his long leg over the back of his horse and jumped down to the dirt path. He patted Ivy's wide neck glistening with sweat. "We rode hard from Mercersburg today, girl. Only stopped in Waynesburg long enough to get a drink at the pump in the Diamond. Can't believe how the town's grown. We'll walk in the rest of the way so you can cool down." He lifted the reins over top of her ears and began leading the horse as he took in scenes of his childhood home. The arched canopy of autumn maples towered above him. *Were the trees this tall and full then? Maybe as a child I never took notice.*

The rushing waters of the east branch of the Antietam at the base of the grassy bank to his left sparked visions of the gristmill's rotating waterwheel upstream. *Jacob – we were always together.*

A few steps down the road, a soft easterly breeze blew under the trees. Ivy caught scent of the sulfurous fumes and jerked her head 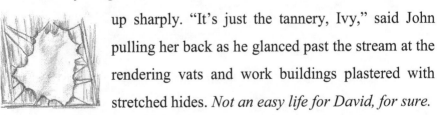 up sharply. "It's just the tannery, Ivy," said John pulling her back as he glanced past the stream at the rendering vats and work buildings plastered with stretched hides. *Not an easy life for David, for sure.*

He shook his head, then turned his sights to the right toward the large barn. "Probably about milking time," he said. A vision of his sisters with seven years of growth since he last saw them flashed through his mind. "Samuel said I'll hardly know them. Susan and Rebecca have both given up their braids for buns. Nan was just one year old when I left – a baby."

Suddenly a sharp barking rang out from the path in front of him. Ivy hesitated as John, hearing the familiar yapping, got down on  his haunches to greet his old friend Mukki eye to eye. The aging golden spaniel halted her staggered dash toward the 'intruders' and quieted as she cautiously extended her nose toward them. "Mukki!" John grinned and spread his arms. "Come here, girl." The dog's feathery tail immediately began to wag furiously and she hobbled headlong into John knocking him to the ground and sending his hat tumbling.

Susan and Rebecca had just lowered their buckets of fresh milk into the cool water of the small stone milk house beside the barn, when they heard Mukki's alarm. Without a word, they hurried out to investigate, taking care to close the heavy door behind them to conserve the cool air. In the same instant, they spied the horse in the lane with a man rolling around in the dirt with their dog. "Who could it be?" asked Rebecca.

John got his feet back under him and stood up, startled to encounter the unexpected stares. He paused only a second. "Susan? Rebecca?" he said.

Susan gasped at the familiar straight, light-brown hair and deep brown eyes, so like her own. Though the voice was that of a man, she knew in a flash this was her brother. "It's John!" She grabbed Rebecca's hand. "Oh, Rebecca, it's John!"

John reached for his hat, brushed the powdery dust from its crown and put it back on. "You're right, Susan – Rebecca." He grinned and picked up Ivy's reins as Mukki scurried around his feet. "It's been a long time, huh? You're all grown up now, both of you."

They rushed to his side and each took hold of an arm. "But, you're taller than Papa!" said Rebecca as they walked toward the house.

Susan spun around in front of her sister and brother to take a long look at him. "John," she repeated. "I see you, but I still don't believe it." Then she frowned slightly. "But you weren't to come 'til the wedding. Why . . .?"

"Well, I see him, too," Rebecca interrupted gazing up past his shoulder. "So it must really be him."

Then Susan stared past John, her eyes following Mukki who had just bolted away down the path again. "And look!" said Susan pointing behind them. "Jacob and Elizabeth have just turned in the lane with the cows. They're back from Snow Hill." She smiled at John as he turned to see.

Bouncing up and down with excitement, Susan determined to take charge of this joyous event. "Rebecca, take John's horse to the barn." Rebecca obediently took Ivy's reins from John as Susan continued, "I'll go fetch Mama and the girls – they're just inside. Papa's all the way up at the mill, so that'll have to wait." As Rebecca moved away, Susan turned to her brother. "John . . . ," she started, but stopped short and hugged him hard before going on, ". . . you can wait here for Jacob and Elizabeth."

"It's all right, Susan," said John laying his hands on her shoulders to quiet her. "I'll be right here. I'm not going anywhere for awhile."

"But it's so exciting, I can't help myself. "It's so . . . so . . . ," At a loss for words, she flashed another smile before speeding away to the house.

As John watched her go, his expression went flat. *If only the news I've brought with me were happy. But it's so sad, so very, very sad.*

-19-

The Changing Tapestry

The special bond between John and Jacob, broken for seven years, reconnected the instant they saw each other. When they met in the lane, they threw their arms around one another and clamped their eyes shut to stop the tears. Jacob's face was buried in John's chest as John's lean frame stretched a full head above Jacob's compact, broad-shouldered body. The time apart had intensified their physical differences. The long-absent brother's face had developed a more chiseled, defined adult quality and a thick beard a shade darker than his fair hair. Jacob's full face appeared even wider framed by a bushier dark beard and full head of curly brunette hair.

Later that day, the family could barely chew their food for smiling at the sight of the two brothers together again at their former places at supper. As the chatter and clatter of the meal subsided, Daniel stood up at the head of the table in the flickering light of the candles and fireplace. Respectful silence followed this gesture, as usual, as every face beamed with gratitude for their papa's rare show

220

of tolerance and affection in having invited John to return to the fold. Even Daniel's usual brusque expression failed to completely disguise his own pleasure at the joyful reunion.

"While we're all together," Daniel pronounced, "John has asked to share his news from Cove Forge – actually from Springfield, now that Samuel's moved his family to their new house." Daniel took his seat, deferring to John who studied his empty plate somberly giving himself time to consider his words. Everyone looked at him anxiously. Despite earlier prodding, he had not yet mentioned his business with anyone, not even Jacob.

God, help me say this well, John prayed silently before he began. He raised his head and surveyed his family with a smile. "First, as you might have suspected, is the good news. The Royer clan up north has a *new* baby to add to their *new* house. Lucy was born, happy and healthy, the day before I left."

"Praise God," murmured Catherine as Daniel nodded approvingly.

"Oh, good," said Nan clapping her hands. "A girl. Now Samuel's boys are outnumbered three-to-two."

John looked at his little sister gently as his smile faded. "Sadly, what I have to share next is difficult." He dropped his eyes, unable to face them as he spoke slowly. "Samuel's Sarah has gone to be with the Lord. After Lucy's birth, the midwife couldn't control the bleeding." John's voice cracked. "Sarah's gone."

No one moved. No one even drew a breath. Their stunned expressions slowly wilted into sadness and disbelief. Finally Catherine whispered, "My poor Samuel. Those poor sweet babies." She raised her head to Daniel, shaking his head slowly at the far end of the table. "We've got to help them, Daniel." He stared blankly at her. "How will they ever manage without Sarah?"

At Daniel's silence, John spoke. "Sarah's mother's with them now. She was there for Lucy's birth and Sarah's . . ." He choked, pressing his fist to his mouth. "She can stay for three or four more weeks, but needs to return to her family in Waynesburg by late October, before the weather turns. Sarah's only sister is married with a husband and three children of her own near Frederick. The Provines have no other women in their family who can help."

Daniel folded his hands in front of him on the table. "Then your mother's right. We have to send someone – one of you girls will go there to help Samuel with the children."

Elizabeth, Susan, Rebecca and even Nan nodded in agreement. Cate covered her mouth to muffle her crying. "Papa, I . . . ," Elizabeth began.

Daniel held up his hand. "Please, let no one speak for now."

"But Papa, I . . ." Elizabeth insisted.

"No, Elizabeth. Be still," he barked. "We must think long and hard about this. We must pray for guidance and consider well who should go before we speak. Too many decisions made in haste are later bound by regret." He glanced at John.

Tears started to glisten in many eyes as the shock set in. No one dared to stir. After a few moments, Daniel coughed lightly. "Today is Friday. We'll speak of this again Sunday evening, not before. *Frau* Provines will care for Samuel's family for now. The Lord will show us the way to help." Daniel stood, his fingers clenching the edge of the table as his arms stiffened for support. "Let our troubled minds be still. We'll come together in our sorrow at devotions tonight and pray for God's guidance in our search for an answer."

Susan ran her hand across the roughly hewn oak mantel over the hearth Henry had completed just days earlier. The mid-afternoon sun laid long rectangles of light across the tightly-packed dirt floor of what would be their kitchen. "Such fine work, Henry." She moved back a step to admire the whole of it. Henry came up behind her and grasped her arms, laying his cheek against the back of her bonnet. "We're so blessed. I . . . I . . . ." She covered her face with her hands as she began to sob.

Henry turned her toward him and wrapped his arms around her. "I can't imagine your family's pain – Samuel's terrible loss. I remember Sarah fondly, though I barely knew her."

Susan looked up at him. "She was a joy, always kind and smiling. They were so happy together." She pressed her head against Henry's chest for a second and then took a seat on a small bench standing against a nearby half-finished wall. Henry sat close beside her and held her hands. She squeezed his calloused fingers. "And what about Rebecca and Elizabeth? What are they to do? How can Rebecca leave George when they're so close to telling Papa they want to be married?" Susan pleaded with Henry. "How can Elizabeth go back to always serving the family with no hope for a husband and little ones of her own, now that she's finally met a man who's touched her heart?" She leaned into Henry crying. "How can we be so fortunate while everyone else suffers so."

Henry rubbed slow circles on Susan's back. "Someone has to go to Springfield to live, to help Samuel with his children. For Elizabeth and Rebecca going up there would be a huge sacrifice. Cate suffers with her illness and Nan's too young." Henry reviewed the predicament Susan had outlined. He studied the fireplace in front of them, mortar seams still moist. "What about us?" Then he waited for the weight of what he'd said to strike Susan.

"What are you saying, Henry?" asked Susan both stunned and puzzled.

224

He turned to her. "Just listen while I think it through out loud. See if this makes some sense to you." He stood up and began pacing as he presented his case. "Why can't we get married and move to Springfield? You've said Samuel has a fine new house, large enough for us to stay with him while I find a place of our own nearby. You could help with the children, especially 'til the newest is stronger. I could almost certainly find work as a mason with the forge there."

"I could ask John. He'd know for sure," Susan offered, catching Henry's excitement.

"I've always loved the mountains." Henry smiled at her. "We share that, you and I. With two older brothers, my home place is already claimed, and moving is the only way to more prosperity and security these days."

He sat beside her again and continued. "Maybe this is an opportunity for all of us. If we go to Huntingdon County, your mother won't have to give up the help she needs at home. Elizabeth and Rebecca can stay close to their loves and we can make an exciting new path together in a new place."

Susan fell back wide-eyed against the wall beam. "But what about our new cabin?" she asked grasping the possibility of Henry's suggestion. "You've done so much work. It's so beautiful." Her eyes stung with bittersweet tears.

"I know I could sell it, as is, to Amos Hess," Henry explained. "He's been helping me with the work and just got engaged to Beatrice

Snyder. He'd take it in a minute, maybe at a small profit. Land's not easy to come by lately."

"And that money could help us with the move," added Susan. She leaned forward. "The move," she repeated. She shook her head. "Oh, Henry. This is all happening so fast. Can we really do this?"

He pulled her up from the bench into his embrace. "We can do anything, anywhere, as long as we're together, Susan. You can ask John about their need for masons. I'll talk to my parents and speak to Amos about the cabin. What do you think?"

"I think I love you," said Susan. She kissed him soundly, pulled back and grinned broadly. They hugged each other hard and rocked back and forth happily joined in the new vision of their future.

"Go forth in God's Name. You are now husband and wife," said Deacon Myers holding Susan and Henry's hands in his as they stood before him with their heads bowed. "Amen." The couple turned to face their families gathered on the threshing floor of the upper level of the Royer barn.

Catherine gazed through her tears at her beautiful daughter, now a wife. *Grown so quickly, so full of love – for everyone. She'll be such a help to Samuel, but I'll miss her so.* She glanced down the bench beside her at her four remaining single daughters. *One blink and they'll be gone as well - all but my Cate.* She sighed.

Despite the rushed celebration, members from both families created quite a crowd for the nuptials. More than 60 siblings, aunts, uncles and cousins joined Susan and Henry's parents in celebrating the young couple's marriage, expressing their sympathies for Sarah's passing and wishing the newlyweds Godspeed on their unexpected journey.

As Susan and Henry linked arms and proceeded down the aisle between the men's and women's sections of seats, the congregants began to rise. Catherine pushed aside her musing and sprang into action. "Girls! Move along to the summer kitchen and get started." She shooed them out the smaller side door of the barn and turned to greet Henry's mother with a warm embrace. "*Frau* Reighart, the Lord has surely blessed our family with a young man as fine as your Henry. I'm so sorry that our misfortune will take him and Susan so far from us. His offer to move to Springfield is more than generous."

Frau Reighart clasped Catherine's hands. "Letting go of a child is never easy, but seeing Henry with your sweet Susan fills the emptiness in my heart. They're both good souls and servants of the Lord. I pray they'll help bring some comfort to Samuel and his family."

"Henry will do well in Springfield," said Daniel as he and Henry's father walked together toward the rear of the barn. "Plenty of work at the forge up north."

Herr Reighart took his black hat from the wall peg and put it on. "More folks moving west and north every day." He smiled at Daniel. "I know your sons have worked hard to make the Springfield Forge successful. Henry's very excited about this move and your son John's been giving him wonderful advice to prepare him."

"And their friend, George Schmucker, has done very well for himself at the forge, too. He was married to our Polly. When we lost her some years ago, not long after they were married, he joined Samuel and John in Huntingdon County. He's since remarried and had a number of children," added Daniel. "Good place to make a home and raise a family."

As they headed outside toward the tables, set up behind the house under a bower of bright October branches, they paused behind  the barn to admire the Conestoga wagon Henry had skillfully bartered for with proceeds from the sale of the cabin to Amos Hess. "Won't be long 'til the wagon's loaded and ready to challenge those mountains," said Henry's father.

"They'll be leaving us next Monday morning with the dawn. John'll be able to guide them. He's made the trip several times, but never with this much cargo. Looks like they're ready to go to housekeeping. The wedding presents will give them a good start," said Daniel.

Herr Reighart rapped his knuckles on the stout sideboards of the wagon bed supporting the arching canvas cover and peered in the back. "Must have had a time getting that 5-plate stove aboard. Quite a wedding gift, *Herr* Royer."

"Almost equal to those fine Kentucky mules you gave them," said Daniel. "They'll need every bit of that muscle to get up those hills. They should be able to cover 15 miles a day."

"Henry said the beasts proved themselves well working at Old Forge. They'll be a fit addition to the Springfield Furnace. And he thinks he'll have no trouble selling this Conestoga to one of the travelers headed even further west than Springfield. John told him there's a real market for these wagons." *Herr* Reighart clapped Daniel on the back.

"Amen," pronounced Daniel concluding the family devotions late that night.

"Amen," echoed the others now joined by Henry Reighart as an official member of the household.

"I've set the hearth in the summer kitchen to a cozy flame," said Rebecca smiling at Susan and Henry. "But before you two settle in, Elizabeth, Cate, Nan and I would like to stop by with our special gifts for you to add to that fine leather traveling bag David gave you and the new mare from Jacob." David and Jacob nodded at the acknowledgement.

"Suppose we could manage that." Susan grinned at Henry who fought hard not to blush. She took his hand and stood as he quickly followed her lead. "We'll go ahead and tidy things 'til you get there."

"*Wundervoll*," squealed Nan as she led the troupe of girls heading out to retrieve their presents.

"*Gute Nacht*," said Susan to those remaining.

"*Ja, gute Nacht*," said Henry.

"Sleep well these next few nights," said Catherine. "'Twill be many a day before you'll feel such comfort again."

Henry had barely stoked the hearth in the summer kitchen when a knock sounded at the door. Susan hugged him. "We have visitors, *mein Mann*."

"*Ist gut, meine Frau*." He kissed her forehead.

Susan opened the door and with a grand bow and sweep of her arm said, "*Wilkommen, meine Schwester*. Have a seat by the fire."

Henry and Susan sat on a low bench by the hooked rug where the girls gathered in a semicircle. Elizabeth presented her gift first, a small book of poems. "Brother Obed from Snow Hill wrote these verses. I hope they give you as much peace in your new home as they have given me."

Susan leafed through the delicate handwritten pages. She held the tiny volume open and showed it to Henry. "It's lovely," she said. "I know how special Snow Hill is to you. I always imagine you with a book in your hand, so this will easily remind me of you every time I see it. Thank you so much, Elizabeth." They embraced and then Elizabeth made way for Rebecca.

"I think you'll remember this magic," said Rebecca handing Susan a small linen pillow with a tiny blue satin bow and delicate stitching that read '*Remember*.' "It's filled with dried lavender - *und fergess-mich-nerts*."

Susan laughed. "Forget-me-nots! How could I forget Oma Stoner's secret? We used these seeds when we were conniving to get Samuel and Sarah together."

Rebecca smiled. "Well, it worked for them. It should work for us, too. To keep us always in each other's hearts." Then she pulled a matching sachet out of her apron pocket. "I made one for myself, too, so I'll not forget you either."

"And George Smith doesn't need any potion to 'remember' you, Rebecca," added Henry.

Rebecca blushed.

Then Cate laid a flat wooden box with a hinged lid on the floor in front of Susan. "Here, *Frau und Herr* Reighart. To help you capture time and thoughts forever."

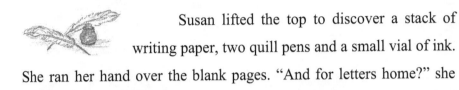 Susan lifted the top to discover a stack of writing paper, two quill pens and a small vial of ink. She ran her hand over the blank pages. "And for letters home?" she said grinning at Cate.

"Of course!" she said. "But I can promise you many letters in return. I have more time for writing now, so you'll know all the news of home and be tempted to pay as many visits as you can."

Nan then leaned in and presented her gift to Susan, a knitted woolen scarf with knotted fringes. "And this will keep you warm on your journeys. I know it's a bit fancy with the trim, but that way you can tell it apart from Henry's." She then produced a second scarf identical to the first, but with plain edges. "Elizabeth helped me stay awake to finish them after we went to bed at night."

Susan cuddled the scarf against her cheek and Henry wrapped his around his neck. "We'll be the warmest travelers on the road," he said.

Cate was the first to extend her arms towards Susan as the five sisters wrapped themselves into a loving huddle. "God has truly blessed me with such fine sisters. I'll miss you every day."

Susan lingered at the open gate of the whitewashed fence surrounding the four-square garden. Nineteen years of memories flitted between the harvested rows of vegetables and bare vines clinging to the posts and pickets. Rosy dawn stretched ribbons across the gray sky and cast a muted, ethereal spell on the scene.

Henry stepped up behind her and rested his hand on her shoulder. "It's time, Susan. Wagon's loaded, mules are harnessed and family's waiting to say goodbye."

"I know." She sighed heavily as she pressed against him. "Just came to gather a bushel of memories before we left."

"Next spring you can plant the seeds for a whole new chapter in a garden of our own. Maybe it won't be as grand as this to start, but I've no doubt one similar to this will crop up near our very own cabin before many seasons pass," Henry reassured her.

As they wandered hand in hand toward the stately stone house, Nan came running up to them. "Mama said for me to fetch you before she changes her mind and begs you to stay. Everyone's working hard to hold off crying 'til you're on your way." Her lower lip started quivering. "It isn't easy."

"How'bout a horsey back ride to the wagon?" said Henry squatting down to offer his back. "You might be too grown up the next time I see you, but not yet."

"As tall as you are, I think it'll still work," said Nan climbing aboard and looping her arms around his neck.

As they approached the others waiting in front of the house, Daniel lifted Nan from Henry's back. "Child, you'll be wearing Henry out before they even get started. He's got a lot of mule power to contend with and lots of miles to cover." He and Henry shared an embrace and the customary kiss of brotherhood between Brethren men. David and Jacob did likewise.

"God be with you, Henry," said Daniel.

"And with you and your family, *Herr* Royer," said Henry.

Susan embraced each of her siblings in turn and then faced her father. Daniel smiled down at her and breathed deeply to contain his emotions. "*Danke*, Papa," she said, "for everything – for a life blessed with security and love." He nodded, unable to risk speaking as he swallowed his tears. They hugged as Catherine quietly wept.

Daniel released her and moved to busy himself with an unnecessary inspection of the mules' harnesses. Susan saw her mother's tears and melted into her arms. "Oh, Mama. I'll miss you so," she whimpered into her mother's shoulder. Catherine pinched her eyes to stop the tears and squeezed Susan as hard as she could.

When they finally parted, Susan held her mother's gaze. "All week long as we packed the wagon and made our plans, I kept remembering what you said to me years ago, when I was so upset about leaving our old cabin to move into the new house. Afraid to let go – afraid of the change. You and I sat by the fire late that night and you said, 'Cherish the past. Anticipate the future. Embrace the present moment.'"

Catherine smiled as she repeated the final phrase together with her daughter, "Give God reverence always."

"I'll try to do all of those things, Mama. Truly I will," said Susan.

"Oma Stoner's words have always served me well. I'm so happy they'll live on in your heart," said Catherine. "Now, Henry, help your wife into this wagon and onto your new life."

"Yes, *Mutter* Royer. Whatever you say." Henry took Susan's elbow, boosted her onto the seat and circled around in front of the 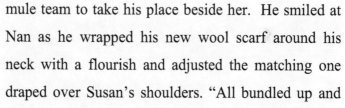 mule team to take his place beside her. He smiled at Nan as he wrapped his new wool scarf around his neck with a flourish and adjusted the matching one draped over Susan's shoulders. "All bundled up and ready to go." He picked up the reins and snapped them sharply as the sturdy animals sprang to life and headed down the dirt lane.

Susan turned, teary-eyed, raising her hand to return her family's waves as she stretched around the open canopy of the wagon so they could see her. Mukki trotted behind them halfway out the lane faster than her advanced years usually allowed yapping her farewell.

Taking one last long look at the stone house and the family who had nurtured her, she whispered, "I love you all." Then she hooked her arm through Henry's as they jostled along, the murmuring Antietam to their right, and made the turn onto the main road heading west.

- Epilogue -

The trilogy of *The Royers of Renfrew*, as a work of historical fiction, is a combination of facts and imagination. Of primary concern is the presentation of the lives of the actual Daniel Royer family who lived in the early 1800s on a farmstead that is now Renfrew Museum and Park in Waynesboro, Pennsylvania. The series has followed paths that members of this family may have taken to arrive at the destinations identified in historical records. What we know of these Royer family members is sketchy. We began with birth and death dates, marriages, names and numbers of children, and some indication where they settled after leaving Waynesburg (now Waynesboro). No diaries or personal accounts of any of the Royer family members are known to exist. Therefore, the portrayal of the personalities, characters and the events depicted in these pages is purely speculation.

The locations included are as historically correct as possible. Records from the Renfrew Museum and accounts from trusted

237

sources about Pennsylvania German farm life and the depiction of Waynesburg and the surrounding area were used extensively in the recreation of their lives. Some license has been taken regarding specific dates to enable the inclusion of historically well-known persons and landmarks in the telling of the story of this hard-working 19th century Pennsylvania German farm family. We hope that in recounting these stories we have conveyed a little of the challenges, hardships, struggles and joys of family life in this bygone era of our region's history.

What follows are some details about a few of the sites where events in our tales unfold and an accounting of what we know happened to the Royers of Renfrew and other historical figures included in our three-volume narrative.

The Daniel Royer Farmstead,
now Renfrew Museum and Park

After the deaths of Daniel Royer (1838), Catherine Stoner Royer (1859) and David Royer (1860), no male heirs of Daniel Royer remained in the Waynesboro area. Daniel and Catherine's youngest child Nancy Royer and husband Alpheus J. Fahnestock purchased two parcels of land from Daniel's once vast holdings at the closing of the estate.

In 1890, Dr. Abraham Strickler of Waynesburg purchased the Royers' farmstead. In 1896, he rebuilt the original barn that had burned replacing it with the Victorian-style barn that now serves as the Renfrew Visitor Center. Prior to 1933 the farmstead was tenant farmed by the Minnick and Beaver families.

In 1943 successful orchardist Edgar A. Nicodemus bought the Royer-Strickler property. He married Emma Geiser and they refurbished and established residence on the property. After the deaths of Edgar Nicodemus (1965) Emma Geiser Nicodemus (1973) and her sister Hazel Geiser, the property was bequeathed to the Borough of Waynesboro.

In 1975, the house and the surrounding 107 acres were opened to the public as Renfrew Museum and Park in accordance with specific instructions included in Emma Nicodemus' will.

Snow Hill Cloister

Known to many as simply "the Nunnery," Snow Hill Cloister, located on Rt. 997, south of Quincy, Pennsylvania, is a collection of buildings that were used by Seventh-Day German Baptists. They formed the religious community in the late 1800's as an off-shoot of the more famous Ephrata Cloister in Lancaster County, Pennsylvania.

Snow Hill derived its name from the Snowberger family who were instrumental in its founding. The congregation, made up of celibate men and women and nearby families, flourished from 1814 until the Civil War. The Seventh-Day German Baptists who celebrated the Sabbath on Saturday were among the many Protestant religious sects who fled to Pennsylvania from religious turmoil and persecution in Europe.

The communal compound operated a farmstead, cooperage, sawmill and gristmill for decades until its eventual decline. Zenobia, the last of the sisters, died in 1894, and the last brother, Obed Snowberger, died in 1895

Old Forge Furnace

In 1811 Holker Hughes of Mont Alto Iron Works constructed two dams and an iron forge near present day Camp Penn. The waterwheel powered by the first dam near the present-day Waynesboro water reservoir on Rattlesnake Run Road powered an up and down sawmill. The second and third waterwheels were located at the second dam that remains today across from present-day Camp Penn. The first wheel ran a forge hammer to crush slag and cinders. The second powered a large bellows house to provide the blast for the furnaces that re-fired the crushed slag to recover an even finer grade of iron.

In 1832 Hughes built a rolling mill and chaffery forge further south, just north of Glen Forney (known as Glen Furney today). In 1835 a nail factory was constructed just south of this operation. This foundry also made the famous Hughes 10-plate stove with a picturesque trademark of a sailing ship under the slogan "Don't give up the ship," a famous quote from a War of 1812 naval battle.

240

At its height, Old Forge employed more than 200 workers. Most of their families lived along Biesecker Gap, on a back road long since abandoned that once ran westward from the forge site across the mountain to the present-day Gap area.

The nail factory was destroyed by fire in 1850. The rolling mill continued operations until 1866 and the forge was completely shut down and razed in 1868. Steam power was replacing waterpower, and the cost of hauling pig iron over the mountains combined with the rundown condition of the properties led to the enterprises' final demise.

Daniel Royer

Daniel Royer was born in 1762, in Lancaster County, Pennsylvania, one of six children to Samuel Royer and Catharine Laubscher. They resided in the Five Forks area near present-day Waynesboro, Pennsylvania. He married Catherine Stoner in 1788 and they had ten children.

In addition to running his farmstead near Waynesburg (now Waynesboro), Daniel served as an ensign in the 5th Company, 1st Battalion of the Cumberland County Militia during the Revolutionary War, as justice of the peace and tax assessor for Washington Township (1786), a Franklin County Court judge, Franklin County commissioner (1791-94) and state legislator in the House of Representatives for 1794-96 and 1799-1800 terms. In 1811 he and his brother, John purchased land in Huntingdon County (now Blair

County) and established an iron ore operation at Cove Forge which grew in later years to become the Springfield Furnace.

He died in 1838 and is interred in the Jacob Mack Cemetery, a field just south of the village of Wayne Heights, immediately east of Waynesboro, Pennsylvania.

Catherine Stoner Royer

Catherine Stoner was born in 1769, the daughter of Abraham and Mary (Miller) Stoner. Her father owned the land which Daniel Royer, who would become her husband, purchased in 1779. She lived on the family farmstead until her death in 1858 and is buried alongside her husband in the Jacob Mack Cemetery.

David Royer

David Royer never married. He resided in the family home and continued to manage the tannery until his death in 1860 at age 70.

Samuel Royer

Samuel Royer married Sarah Provines, the daughter of a Waynesburg barrel maker, in 1816 and they had six children. Sarah died in 1832 after their move to Huntingdon County. In 1835 Samuel married Martha (Patton) McNamara who had four children from a previous marriage. Samuel and Martha had four children for a total of 14 children in the household. He became an influential ironmaster and businessman and served at the State Constitutional Convention of 1837. By 1843 Samuel had overextended his finances by investing in a rolling mill at Portage Iron Works and a canal transfer company. These investments, in addition to a decline of the importance of the iron ore industry, resulted in his financial ruin and bankruptcy. However, he sold the Springfield Furnace operation that totaled 14,222 acres to family members. Heirs of Daniel Royer controlled the furnace until 1885. Samuel died in 1856 at age 64 and is buried in Huntingdon County, Pennsylvania.

Elizabeth Royer Good

Elizabeth Royer married David Good in 1826. They became Lutherans and had seven children, six of whom survived to adulthood. All of the children were born in Franklin County, but the family moved to Huntingdon County sometime after 1840 when David purchased the Springfield Furnace operation from his brother-in-law, Samuel, who had fallen on hard economic times. She died in 1868 at age 74. One of her sons served as a doctor in the Union Army during the Civil War.

Mary "Polly" Royer Schmucker

Mary "Polly" Royer Schmucker married George Schmucker in 1819. Various death dates are recorded for her. *Antietam Ancestors*, a publication of the Waynesboro Historical Society indicates that she died just one year after her marriage. However, records on file with the Royer Museum in Williamsburg, Pennsylvania list her husband, George Schmucker as having seven children with "his wife Mary Royer" after his move to Cove Forge to join his brothers-in-law at the ironworks sometime after 1820. For those enchanted by our portrayal of Polly's vibrant personality, there's hope that she did not die in childbirth a year after her marriage, but enjoyed a full life and the arrival of six more children with her beloved George.

Susan Royer Reighart

Surprisingly little is known about what became of Susan Royer, the heroine of our story. She did, indeed, marry Henry Reighart, although the date of the wedding is unknown. They had two children and moved to Huntingdon County (date unknown) where they later died (dates unknown).

Rebecca Royer Smith

Rebecca Royer married George Smith in 1831. They eventually moved to Huntingdon County. Children and death dates are unknown.

Jacob Royer

Jacob Royer never married. He resided in the family home and continued operation of the family gristmill on the Royer farmstead until his death in 1852 at age 52. He is buried in the Jacob Mack Cemetery.

John Royer

John Royer never married. He was sent to Cove Forge at an early age (date unknown) to clerk for his uncle, who was also named John Royer. In 1839, he and his brother-in-law George Schmucker invested in the Springfield Furnace operation. He died in 1885 at the age of 87.

Cate Royer

Her given name was Catharine, Jr. She never married and lived on the family farmstead until her death in 1883 at age 76. Of interest is the fact that Catharine, Jr. is the only one of Daniel and Catherine's ten children who was not listed as an inheritor of any part of the family estate. Unlike her siblings, neither a day nor month is listed with her birth date.

Nancy Royer Fahnestock

Nancy Royer married Peter Fahnestock in 1849 at age 37. Peter was the son of Andrew Fahnestock, who served as an elder for many years at Snow Hill Cloister. They had one son, Alpheus J. Fahnestock. Nancy inherited her mother's personal estate in 1854. After Catherine Royer's death in 1859, Nancy purchased two parcels of land from what was left of the estate. The family remained on the farmstead along with Nancy's sister, Catherine, Jr. until the death of both her husband and sister in 1883. She then moved to Philadelphia to live with her son Alpheus and his wife Malinda Frantz where she died in 1898 at age 86.

George Schmucker

George Schmucker was born in Waynesburg, Pennsylvania in 1792. Records show his father was a Lutheran minister, but little else is known of his family. He married Mary (Polly) Royer in 1819. He moved to Huntingdon County, Pennsylvania. and invested in the Springfield Furnace operations with his brothers-in-law John and Samuel Royer in 1839. Records from the Royer Museum in Williamsburg, Pennsylvania identify him as the father of seven children to "wife Mary Royer." Death date is unknown.

Israel Baer and Mollie Null Baer

Israel Baer (1826-82) and Mary "Mollie" Null (1823-96) were married in 1856 and later moved from Waynesboro to Ashland, Ohio. Records list Mollie as being "reared by Peter Fahnestock." Before leaving the Waynesboro area, Israel Baer worked at the Royer gristmill at various times between 1849 and 1866.

Israel and Mollie had six children. They named their first child Franklin Royer Baer, presumably out of respect for the Royer family and their Franklin County connection – strong evidence that their memories of Pennsylvania were positive. They are both buried in Ashland Cemetery, Ashland, Ohio.

**Note: Their first child, Franklin Royer Baer married a daughter of the Van Duren family of Ohio who had become millionaires in the iron industry. This was certainly a giant step from his mother's roots just a generation earlier as a "swamper" and foster child in Waynesburg.

Peter Lehman

Peter Lehman, known as "Father of Snow Hill," was born in 1757. He died in 1823 and is buried in Snow Hill's cemetery.

Andrew "Andreas" Fahnestock

Andrew Fahnestock, born 1781, learned his German Seventh-Day Baptist doctrine from Peter Lehman (originally from the Ephrata

Cloister), and was considered the logical successor upon Lehman's death in 1823. Fahnestock served Snow Hill as Prior for 17 years. He usually traveled on foot on his many journeys to the dwindling parent church, and was a picturesque character with a flowing white beard as he made many journeys between the two cloisters carrying a long staff and wearing a long drab coat and white broad-brimmed hat. In addition to his religious calling, Andrew Fahnestock was a weaver, a farmer and invented a pump which sold for $14.50. He married Margaret Graver and had seven children. He died in 1863 at age 81. They are both buried in Snow Hill's cemetery.

Obed Snowberger

The last of the male Solitaries of Snow Hill, Obed was born in 1823 and lived his entire life at Snow Hill. In addition to a body of poetry, he wrote articles for their religious paper and, as a musician, played the piano, organ and accordion and wrote a song called *Snow Hill Quickstep*. Among his manuscripts are neatly written scores for hymns including *When I Survey the Wondrous Cross*. He was also a mechanic making repairs to the mill, fixing clocks and operating a small printing press. He died in 1895 at age 72. His obituary stated he was "a great reader, well posted on current subjects and philosophy, an original thinker . . . kind, benevolent and everywhere loved."

Although he and his poetry are mentioned in connection with Elizabeth Royer's imagined sojourn at the Snow Hill Cloister, Obed would have been born shortly after her time there.

Melonia (born Lydia Mentzer)

Both Melonia and Zenobia (born Elizabeth Fyock, died 1894, age 83) were indeed some of the sisters who lived at "the Nunnery." Melonia who joined the order at the age of 17 was reported to have suffered terribly from what may have been crippling arthritis and died at age 41 in March 1860, which would have made her a child of three at the time of her fictionalized friendship with Elizabeth Royer.

Melonia is buried in "God's Acre" just north of Snow Hill, but the inscription we attribute to her gravestone is borrowed from the epitaph Brother Obed Snowberger wrote for his own marker at the Snow Hill cemetery prior to his death in 1895.

The Daniel Royer Family

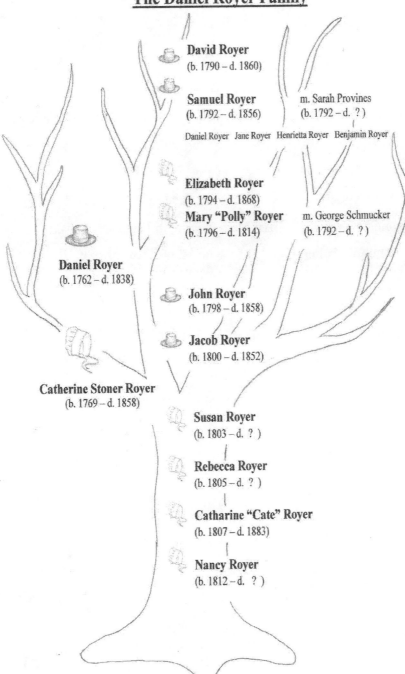

David Royer
(b. 1790 – d. 1860)

Samuel Royer   m. Sarah Provines
(b. 1792 – d. 1856)   (b. 1792 – d. ?)

Daniel Royer   Jane Royer   Henrietta Royer   Benjamin Royer

Elizabeth Royer
(b. 1794 – d. 1868)

Mary "Polly" Royer   m. George Schmucker
(b. 1796 – d. 1814)   (b. 1792 – d. ?)

Daniel Royer
(b. 1762 – d. 1838)

John Royer
(b. 1798 – d. 1858)

Jacob Royer
(b. 1800 – d. 1852)

Catherine Stoner Royer
(b. 1769 – d. 1858)

Susan Royer
(b. 1803 – d. ?)

Rebecca Royer
(b. 1805 – d. ?)

Catharine "Cate" Royer
(b. 1807 – d. 1883)

Nancy Royer
(b. 1812 – d. ?)

Glossary

agape meal	-	Love Feast
aggravate	-	to make worse or more severe
amble	-	to walk at a relaxed pace
ample	-	plentiful, abundant
board (n.)	-	table spread with a meal
bodice	-	upper part of a dress
board and batten	-	wall with alternating broad and narrow boards
bosh sweep	-	tool used in maintenance of iron furnace
brawn	-	muscular strength
broadsheet	-	newspaper
burdock	-	wild plant with small, prickly burrs
breeches	-	pants fitting snuggly at hem just below knees
brusquely	-	abruptly; harshly
buttress (n.)	-	structure to stabilize a wall or building
calloused	-	thickened skin due to hard labor
canopy	-	a cover suspended above an area
cavernous	-	like a cavern
celibacy	-	the state of not being married
chaff	-	light husk easily separated from seed
chamber pot	-	a bowl kept in the bedroom and used as a toilet
chew	-	chewing tobacco
cloister	-	a house of persons living under religious vows
collier	-	one that produces charcoal
comely	-	attractive
communal	-	used or shared in common with others

communion	-	Christian sacrament to honor Christ's death
copse	-	a grove of small trees or high brush
covey	-	small flock or group
damask	-	strong, patterned fabric often used for linens
deference	-	humble submission and respect
demure	-	modest, serious
discordant	-	quarrelsome
disorient	-	confuse
distraught	-	troubled by doubt or mental conflict
dormant	-	sleeping; sluggish
dormitory	-	a building providing rooms for sleeping
douse	-	to drench or throw liquid on
dregs	-	sediment in a liquid
euphoria	-	feeling of well-being; joy
excursion	-	a trip, usually for pleasure
feign	-	to pretend
fixated	-	focused attention
flax	-	plant whose fibers are used to make linen
fodder	-	food for cattle or horses
forage	-	(v.) to wander in search of (n.) food for animals
formidable	-	strong, having qualities to discourage approach
footer	-	heavy corner foundations for building
gelding	-	a castrated male horse
gluttonous	-	excessively eating or drinking
gnarled	-	deformed; twisted
gourd	-	hard melon often hollowed for use as a vessel

gregarious	-	friendly; sociable
Goliath	-	Biblical giant killed by David with a sling
gristmill	-	a mill for grinding grain
harrumph	-	a huffing sound of disgust
hillock	-	a small hill
homespun	-	rough cloth made of wool or linen
immodest	-	indecent or improper
indentured	-	bound by contract to work for another person
influx	-	a flowing in
intrigue	-	engage in plotting or trickery
Kist	-	large chest for household items; hope chest
laudanum	-	strong opium extract used as painkiller
liniment	-	a medicinal ointment for application to the skin
lintel	-	horizontal piece supporting top of an opening
lope	-	an easy step or walking style
lurid	-	gruesome, ghastly
mason	-	skilled workman who builds with stone
melee	-	a confused struggle
midwife	-	a woman trained to assist in childbirth
mill (v.)	-	1. to grind 2. to move about aimlessly
millrace	-	canal for water flowing to and from mill wheel
mottled	-	having colored spots or blotches
muslin	-	a rough cotton fabric
ornery	-	irritable; stubborn
pallet	-	straw-filled mattress; small, hard bed
palpable	-	able to be felt or touched

patriarch	-	the father or founder
pig iron	-	crude iron direct product of a blast furnace
pious (adj.)	-	devoutly religious
plague (n.)	-	pestilence, widespread disease
pneumonia	-	disease of the lungs
pommel	-	knob at the front of a saddle
pox	-	a disease characterized by blistering sores
precarious	-	uncertain, possibly dangerous
predicament	-	difficult situation; dilemma
pulsate	-	to throb or beat
pulverize	-	to grind into small particles
purgatory	-	a state or place of temporary punishment
quarried	-	dug from an open excavation or mine
rambunctious	-	unruly; full of uncontrolled energy
reconciliation	-	a settling of differences or disputes
render	-	use harsh chemicals to break down
rhubarb	-	plant with thick, large leaves and reddish stems
rounders	-	child's game resembling baseball
Sabbath	-	a day observed as sacred
salvage (v.)	-	to save or rescue property in danger
sassafras	-	American tree related to the laurel family
saturated	-	soaked; filled to capacity with moisture
scored	-	marked by scratches, grooves or lines
scrip	-	paper currency used for exchange of goods
shanty	-	small, crudely built shelter or home
shirk	-	avoid

smelling salts	-	strong smelling mixture to revive senses
smolder	-	burn slowly, without flame
snitzen party	-	fall event centered around apple butter making
soapwort	-	wild plant with tiny, fragrant white flowers
sojourn	-	a temporary stop or stay
sop (v.)	-	to soak up or mop up
swath	-	(n.) a long strip of cloth
staple	-	something used or needed constantly
strapping	-	strong, robust
sulfurous	-	noxious; scent like burning sulfur
tenant	-	one who rents or leases a property
tether	-	a leather strap that fastens or controls animals
torturous	-	very difficult; cruelly painful
tottering	-	unstable
towhead	-	a person having soft, whitish hair
translucent	-	partly transparent; shining or glowing
unleavened	-	baked without yeast
unobtrusive	-	not obvious or aggressive; inconspicuous
venison	-	meat from a deer
victuals	-	food; provisions
wend	-	to travel slowly or by an indirect route

Recipes for Featured Dishes

Cherry Knepplies

1 quart pitted sour cherries
1 cup water
3 tablespoons cornstarch
Sugar to taste

2 cups flour
2 eggs
¾ cup milk
2/3 teaspoon salt

Bring cherries to boil.
Combine cornstarch and water to make a paste.
Add paste to cherries and cook until thickened, stirring constantly.
Remove from heat, but keep warm.
To make knepplies, sift flour and salt together.
Make a well in the flour and add eggs.
Stir with a fork and add milk to mixture.
Stir until a smooth, thick batter is formed.
Drop batter into 1 ½ quarts of boiling salt water by tilting bowl at an angle so that batter comes just to the edge of the bowl. As it is about to drop off into salt water, cut it with the side of a spoon so that about ½ a teaspoon of batter drops at once. Every fourth or fifth time, dip spoon into boiling water to keep batter from sticking to spoon.
Let boil for one minute after all the batter is in the kettle.
Remove from heat and drain through colander.
Melt ½ cup of butter and let it brown.
Pour brown butter over knepplies.
To serve, pour thickened cherries over little balls of dough.

Rhubarb Pudding

3 slices bread
1 cup diced rhubarb
1/3 cup brown sugar
1/8 teaspoon nutmeg
1 tablespoon butter

For custard:
1 egg
¼ cup sugar
1 cup milk

Cut bread in small cubes.
Place half of bread cubes in greased baking dish.
Then add rhubarb and sprinkle with sugar and nutmeg.
Top with remaining bread crumbs and dot with butter.
Beat egg. Add sugar and milk.
Pour mixture over contents of baking dish.
Bake at 350 for approximately 40 minutes or until a knife comes out
    clean when inserted in pudding.
Serve warm or cold with rich milk or cream.

Serves 6.

Apple Brown Betty

2 cups tart apple, diced
1 ½ cups soft bread crumbs
2/3 cup brown sugar
¼ cup butter, melted

¼ teaspoon salt
1 teaspoon cinnamon
2 tablespoons lemon juice
1/3 cup water

Add melted butter to bread crumbs.
Combine apples, sugar, salt and cinnamon.
Place a layer of buttered crumbs in bottom of greased casserole.
Add a layer of diced apples and another of crumbs.
Continue with alternate layers, having bread crumbs on top.
Combine lemon juice and water and pour over mixture.
Bake at 350 for 1 hour.

Serves 6.

Apple Butter Cake

½ cup shortening
1 cup sugar
4 eggs, beaten
2 ½ cups flour
1 ½ teaspoons soda
½ teaspoon salt

1 teaspoon cinnamon
½ teaspoon cloves
½ teaspoon nutmeg
1 cup sour milk or buttermilk
1 cup apple butter

Cream the shortening.
Add the sugar gradually and continue to cream until fluffy.
Add well-beaten eggs and mix thoroughly.
Sift flour; measure and sift again with salt, soda and spices.
Add dry ingredients alternately with sour milk.
Add apple butter and blend well into mixture.
Pour into greased loaf pan 5x9x4 inches.
Bake at 350 for 45 to 50 minutes.

Cottage Cheese Pie

1 ½ cups cottage cheese
½ cup sugar
2 tablespoons flour
¼ teaspoon salt

2 eggs, separated
¼ cup cinnamon or nutmeg
2 cups milk
pastry for one pie crust

Combine cottage cheese, sugar, flour, salt and spice.
Add beaten eggs yolks and mix thoroughly.
Add milk gradually to make a smooth paste.
Fold in beaten egg whites.
Pour into unbaked pastry shell.
Bake at 350 for 1 hour.

Bread Pudding

2 cups bread cubes   3 tablespoons butter
2 cups milk   1 teaspoon vanilla
¼ cup sugar   ½ teaspoon cinnamon (optional)
2 eggs   ¼ teaspoon nutmeg (optional)
½ teaspoon salt

Use bread a day old. Cut into cubes ¼ inch square.
Place cubes of bread in a buttered baking dish.
Scald milk and add butter and sugar.
Pour scalded milk over beaten eggs and mix thoroughly.
Then pour mixture over bread cubes and blend together.
Set baking dish in a pan of hot water.
Bake at 350 for about 1 hour or until a knife comes out clean when
    inserted in center.
Serve hot or cold with heavy milk or cream.

Serves 6.

Pan Haus
(Scrapple)

(As posted at the Fahnestock House at Renfrew Park)

Take a pig's haslet (heart, liver and other edible organs) and as much offal (entrails), lean and fat pork as you wish to make scrapple. Boil them together in a small quantity of water until they are tender; chop them fine. After taking them out of the liquor, season as sausage. Then skim off the fat that has arisen where the meat was boiled, throw away the water, put the ingredients back in the pot, thickening with half buckwheat and half Indian (cornmeal). Let it boil, and then pour into pans to cool. Slice and fry in sausage fat.

About the Authors

Marie Lanser Beck is a former journalist and historian who has written and edited two volumes of veterans' stories and assisted Sen. Edward W. Brooke in writing his memoirs (*Bridging the Divide: My Life*, Rutgers University Press, 2007).

Maxine Beck has a bachelor's degree in education and a master's degree in English. She is a former high school teacher with 17 years of experience teaching advanced English and writing. She has also authored a novel *Chagrin Falls* and a humorous memoir *Tripping to London . . . and Life.*

Both have been associated with Renfrew Institute for Cultural and Environmental Studies in Waynesboro, Pennsylvania for many years. Marie has served on the board of directors of the Renfrew Museum and Park, as well as the Renfrew Institute. Maxine currently serves as president of the Renfrew Institute's Board of Directors.

About Renfrew Museum and Park

Renfrew Museum and Park in Waynesboro, Pennsylvania preserves the Royer farmstead and interprets Pennsylvania German farm life on a 107-acre site not far from the Mason-Dixon Line, 65 miles from Washington, D.C. and Baltimore, Maryland. The Royer Family's 1812 stone farmhouse and several of the outbuildings described in *The Royers of Renfrew* have been preserved and are open to the public.